Also by Alan Gibbons

An Act of Love
The Edge
End Game
Hate
Raining Fire
The Trap

The Legendeer Trilogy

Shadow of the Minotaur
Vampyr Legion
Warriors of the Raven

THEY SAW TOO MUCH

ALAN GIBBONS

Orion
Children's Books

First published in Great Britain in 2018 by
Hodder and Stoughton

1 3 5 7 9 10 8 6 4 2

A CIP catalogue record for this book
is available from the British Library.

ISBN 978 1 7806 2248 4

Typeset by Input Data Services Ltd, Somerset

Printed and bound by CPI Group (UK) Ltd, Croydon, CR0 4YY

The paper and board used in this book are from
well-managed forests and other responsible sources.

MIX
Paper from
responsible sources
FSC® C104740

Orion Children's Books
An imprint of
Hachette Children's Group
Part of Hodder and Stoughton
Carmelite House
50 Victoria Embankment
London EC4Y 0DZ

An Hachette UK Company

www.hachette.co.uk
www.hachettechildrens.co.uk

To the 96.
In memory of the victims of the Hillsborough disaster.

HOME

It all came down to the sins of the father. That's what it was all about. Yes, good old Dad, he screwed everything up, very nearly got me killed. You don't normally give death much thought at my age. When you're sixteen, you're not supposed to be obsessed with mortality, life after death, death after life. You've got enough on your plate just making it through the day, getting your head straight about relationships, the meaning of life, what to choose at Nando's, the exam rollercoaster, without having to worry about death too. I've learned a thing or two in the last year, though.

Lesson one: life is a tragedy. It always ends the same way. That Grim Reaper guy, he can come quietly, slipping out of the shadows without a sound. There's no fanfare, no ominous *Jaws* theme. There's no telltale sickle set jauntily over his shoulder, no cloak and hood, just a breath of dark wind and he's standing right next to you, sizing you up for a wooden box. He made his appearance one night on the sands in front of our house, a half-renovated beachside

1

property in Crosby. It was the place my parents chose as a refuge to escape whatever it was they were running from.

Down there on the beach, in the dimming light. I was with the girl who turned my life upside down; I thought at the time it was in a good way. Her name was Ceri. A sharp gust from the sea tore her words away as we walked, scattering them like raindrops. She felt me tug her sleeve and turned towards me. She had these heart-stopping, hazel eyes. She always looked kind of startled and anxious. Every time I think about her, that's the image I see.

Startled.

Anxious.

The lost girl.

I suppose we were both lost, each in our own particular way.

"Sorry," I said. "I didn't hear what you said."

"Tears in the wind. It looks like rain."

That brought a smile to my face. Ceri James had a way with words. Tears in the wind, not drizzle. I watched her rich mane of coppery hair whipping round her pale skin and freckled cheeks and I liked what I saw. I had never been the kind to get serious over any one girl. Girls like me. I like them. Fun is the name of the game. Then there was Ceri. I mean, nobody could accuse her of being fun! No way. She put the *oo* into gloomy. That didn't stop me being deeply attracted to her. An addiction, that's what she was. I wanted her to be more than a short-term thing. Those vivid hazel eyes met mine and I held her look for the longest time, smiling, willing her to smile back. She didn't. That was Ceri. The Gloomy Girl.

"So what do you think?" she asked.

I thought she was amazing, but that's not what she was asking.

"Do we get our photos now or come back when the weather's better?"

I turned the camera on the wide, open sands and the rolling tide, the Seaforth docks and the slowly revolving windmills. This was the fantastic view I saw every morning when I drew my curtains.

Ceri wasn't my usual type. The girls I usually went for were, what shall we say, fine. Call me shallow, but I pursued the ones every guy wanted to be seen with, the lookers, right shape, right make-up, right image. OK, I admit it, I liked seeing the jealous looks in the other guys' eyes. This thing with Ceri was different, though. She wasn't one of the popular girls at all. You wouldn't pick her out in a crowd. The first time I tried to chat her up, I cracked a joke, something about gingers being the UK's oppressed minority. That went well! She gave me a look that could curdle milk. I made a mental note not to go there again.

"Well?"

"We're here, aren't we? Let's get on with it."

I weighed the camera in my right hand. It was a quality piece of kit and I'd been carrying it around as if it were made of cut glass. It was brave of Mrs Abrahams to put Dyspraxia Boy in charge of something like this. I could

3

fall over my own shadow. She was either very trusting or very stupid.

I nudged Ceri with my elbow. "What's a bit of rain between friends?"

OK, so we weren't exactly friends. If I'm honest, we were little more than strangers, thrown together by chance. I was new to the school and Ceri wasn't the type to make the first move. We were meant to work together on prep for our Art GCSE. That's right, Art, the subject the government thinks is a waste of time. I've never been much good at the academic stuff, can't get my head round it to be honest, but I can draw. Anyway, back to Ceri. I tell you straight, I wanted to get to know her better. One look at her, and I felt hot under the collar. It wasn't going to be easy. Ceri James was hard to approach, harder still to know. She wrapped herself in a bubble of silence and guarded looks. I don't remember her having many friends. Make that *any* friends.

The things I learned about her came and went the way noises came and went here on the Mersey shore, transported away on the wind in fugitive, fleeting snatches of sound, turbulence and rumour. Playground equipment would clang, waves rush, seagulls yelp, then the wind would override them all with its wild, throaty roar.

I trained the camera lens on Ceri. She was slight, delicate even, so tiny you'd think the breeze might whip her away. I let the camera roam then focused on her pinched, bewitching features. She frowned and pulled her hair across her face, making an auburn slash across her blanched cheeks.

"Don't do that," she scolded, without an atom of humour.

"Why? Everybody likes having their picture taken."

The scowl deepened into a dark cloud behind the veil of reddish hair.

"Well, I don't."

I laughed and pointed the lens at her again. Her thin arm flashed at me.

"Give me that!"

Ceri snatched at the camera.

"Hey, careful. You're going to break it, you muppet. It doesn't belong to us."

The camera belonged to the Art Department. We were meant to take a series of photos of the Antony Gormley statues, *Another Place*. If you don't know it, *Another Place* is one of Liverpool's top tourist attractions, scores of cast-iron figures that keep their ghostly vigil on the beach that stretches from the north end of the docks up towards Southport. I watch them from my windows most nights, when I'm on my own and the demons come calling. The series of photos was going to be the basis of a portfolio of work.

"Delete that photo now."

"OK, OK, I'm doing it. Who pushed your cranky button?" My good humour had ebbed a little. Prickly didn't come close to describing Ceri when she was in this mood. "I'm only trying to have a laugh. What's the matter with you?"

Ceri's eyes blazed with indignation.

"There's nothing the matter with me. You just ask my permission before you take my picture. Got that?"

Her eyes flashed. She meant it. Really meant it. I held up my hands, wondering why she was making such a big deal of everything.

"Got it." I wrinkled my nose. "Jeez. What a drama queen."

I half expected my words to trigger another outburst, but Ceri had already moved on, her attention drawn to the gleaming, blue Lincoln that was pulling into the car park. It was some car, a sleek American sedan. The owner liked his cars, that much was clear. I heard the tyres rumble on the tarmac and turned, following the direction of her gaze. The Lincoln was all alloys and body vents, a petrol head's vehicle of choice. The owner must have spent hours customising his pride and joy.

"You don't see many of those around," I commented.

"If you say so. I'm not interested in cars."

The way I saw it, if you weren't interested in cars, you weren't interested in life. A seagull keened overhead, hanging on the wind, pale and fleeting against the fading light of the September evening. There were two men in the car. I had a bad feeling about them right from the start. I'd been around hard men all my life. So I watched. The driver killed the engine and they remained sitting in the vehicle, staring straight ahead at the marina. They didn't speak, didn't exchange glances. I wouldn't say their behaviour set off alarms, but they had my attention. They seemed to be oblivious to our presence as we stood on the path that led down on to the beach. I lodged the camera on top of a bin and flipped open the LCD monitor screen.

"What are you doing?"

"Getting a picture."

"What's with the monitor?"

I demonstrated.

"They won't know I'm snapping them." I completed my explanation. "If I look through the viewfinder, I'm only going to draw attention to myself."

"Why do you want their picture anyway?"

I don't think I even knew myself. I just had this feeling.

"Dunno," I said. "Don't you want to know what they're up to?"

Ceri didn't share my curiosity. "They're killing time. It's a free country."

The driver lowered his window and lit a cigarette, grey smoke dissipating into the gathering dusk. That was the first time I saw him, the killer. The lighter flared for a moment, illuminating his features. I zoomed in to get a close up. The guy's face was almost fleshless, cheekbones high and prominent, scalp shaven. He had a distinctive snake tattoo slithering up his neck. The man in the passenger seat remained in shadow, but he was shorter, running to fat. Running nothing. He'd got there already, breasting the tape with his flabby arms thrown out wide.

"Let's see," Ceri said, peering at the LCD monitor. It was the taller man with the tattoo who commanded her attention. "Ugh, I don't like the look of him."

"I'm with you there. He fell right out of the Ugly Tree."

She put her hand in the way of the lens.

"Will you just stop? Mrs Abrahams is going to wonder what the Gruesome Brothers are doing on her memory card."

"I'll delete the shots before I return the camera."

Ceri gave me a long look.

"So why bother taking them in the first place?"

I ignored her. Like I said before, I don't know why I was so interested myself. Imagine if I had known then what I do now. Killing time. What a horribly accurate choice of words. I nodded in the direction of the beach.

"We should make a move. We don't want to lose the light."

Ceri glanced at her phone, registering the time.

"There's no need to panic. It's only six o'clock. We've got an hour before the light goes."

I was already walking. There was a troubled sky that evening. The beach was starkly beautiful. I liked the seashore, with its sense of wilderness and space, so different to the inner city neighbourhood where I was raised. I didn't like having to move out of Liverpool 8, but I did like the view from our new house. Ceri hurried to keep up.

"Slow down," she said. "You've got longer legs than me."

The average Dachshund had longer legs than Ceri. I was tempted to call her short-arse, you know, affectionately, but I resisted the temptation. I mean, I wanted her to like me so why queer the pitch with another stupid remark? I glanced over my shoulder.

"Is the car still there?"

Ceri stopped, turned and strained to see.

"Yes, but I don't know what they're doing."

Everything about these guys screamed trouble.

"Beats me, but they're up to no good. I know the type."

"What type is that, John?" she asked, clearly intrigued.

I'd got her attention. Mistake. I didn't want her becoming too interested in my past.

"Trust me," I told her. "Whatever they're doing here, it isn't legit."

Ceri scrutinised the vehicle. I continued along the path past the pond where waterfowl were gathered, coming over in anticipation of being fed. I lingered for a moment.

"Sorry guys. Nothing for you today. I'm all out of goodies."

Ceri caught up.

"They don't understand you, you know. Birds have brains the size of walnuts."

"They understand me. I'm a regular Dr Dolittle."

"Well, just wait for me, will you, Dr Dolittle? I'm calling Gemma."

"Gemma?"

9

"My best mate. I showed you her picture."

That's right, she had, but I didn't take much notice. Gemma was pretty unremarkable, mousey-haired, slightly chubby, glasses. What was to tell?

"She's at the same kids' home as you, right?"

"Was. She left Greenways last year."

She made the call and was about to speak when she lurched forward. Some guy had just slammed into her from behind. I clocked his features in a second, black guy, kind of wiry and powerful-looking, dreads fading to grey.

"Hey, watch it," I warned him. "Haven't you got any manners?"

Then he did the strangest thing. He hung on to me, fingers clawing at my jacket, and mumbled something. His words were slurred and incoherent. Alchy. At least, that's what I thought.

"Come again?"

His face was taut, his expression kind of desperate. He tried to get his words out, but as he looked over my shoulder his eyes widened and he stumbled off without a word, half running. He had his arms hugging his ribs, as if he had stomach ache.

"Hey, I'm talking to you?" I stared at Ceri. "What do you make of that?"

"Just leave it," she said. "What did he say to you?"

I shrugged. "Couldn't understand a word he said. Got to be a drunk, or a druggie." Mr Empathy, that's me.

"So you don't know him?"

10

That made me laugh.

"Why should I know him?"

Then I got it. Two black males. They've got to know each other, haven't they?

"What, the colour of my skin means I'm supposed to know every black guy in Liverpool? How does that work?"

Ceri shook her head.

"I didn't mean anything by it." She looked embarrassed. "Forget it, OK. Let's take these photos and go. There's something weird about this evening."

I nodded. "Who's arguing?"

Funny thing, as we walked on, the stumbling man's face floated through my mind. There was something kind of familiar about him. We followed through the gap in the dunes and the beach opened up before us, bleak, desolate and magnificent. A container ship was gliding across the bay, heading out from the Mersey into the Irish Sea. It was silhouetted against the garish sunlight, reduced to little more than an abstract shape in the murk.

"It looks so close," Ceri said, breaking her silence. "You'd think it would run aground."

I found myself wondering out loud. "Where do you think it's going?"

"Germany, the Netherlands, anywhere really. Why?"

"My dad's working abroad. Doha."

"Where's that?"

"It's in one of those Arab kingdoms in the Gulf. Qatar."

11

"Catarrh? I thought that was nasal congestion." A pause. "What does he do out there?"

"Construction. He's a spark."

She looked puzzled.

"Electrician," I explained.

"So say electrician."

She screwed up her eyes.

"Your dad, do you miss him?"

Stupid question.

"Of course."

Way to go, John lad, there wasn't even a stumble as you delivered the line. You disguised it well.

"Is that why you're minted?"

That got a laugh.

"What makes you think we're rich?"

Ceri glanced at the nearby houses.

"Beachfront property. That's got to cost."

I wondered for a moment why it mattered where I lived then I remembered Ceri was in care. I found myself wondering if she had anyone to miss. The home where she lived was half a mile from my house. I knew that much. Did she have family? I was starting to realise how little I knew about her. It was time to move the conversation on. With somebody as touchy as Ceri, you have to be careful what buttons to press.

"Let's take some shots. That sky is fantastic."

I changed the settings and peered through the viewfinder.

"I love the iron men, don't you?"

The Gormley statues were keeping their shadowy watch on the bay, motionless sentries in the grainy twilight.

"We should get their faces," Ceri suggested.

"What faces? They don't have any."

Ceri wasn't having it.

"Yes, they do. Their skin is peeling. They're like lepers."

"Not very PC, that."

"So what are you supposed to say? Their skin is all scabby."

"That's just the way they're rusting."

Ceri was stubborn.

"They're still scabby." She wandered round the nearest statue. "Scabby, scabby statue." She tapped it on the nose. "That means . . . you."

A sudden gust of wind made patterns on the beach.

"Like a rattlesnake," I noted, watching the dry sand from the dunes zigzagging across the darker, damper mud beneath my feet.

Ceri wasn't interested in the rattlesnake. She'd seen something.

"Hey, one of the statues just moved."

I was distracted, flicking through the stuff I'd taken so far. I didn't even look up as I thumbed through the pictures, nodding briefly at some, frowning at others.

"Yeah, right."

I deleted another blurry image.

"It's true, I tell you." Ceri insisted. "See for yourself."

I had my gaze firmly fixed on the viewfinder.

"You're imagining things."

Ceri poked me in the ribs.

"Yes? So what do you say about *him*?"

She was referring to the short, painfully thin man staggering along the shoreline a couple of hundred metres away. I recognised the stumbling, shambling gait and the dreads as they tossed in the wind.

"That's the moron who barged into you."

Ceri strained to see.

"I think you're right."

"It's him."

The guy turned his face up to the sky, kind of dreamy and distracted.

Ceri squinted into the gloom. "I knew there was something wrong when he bumped into us. John, I think he's hurt."

I used the zoom to follow his progress. It was the same as before. He had his arms wrapped round his ribs. He removed his hand from his side and stared at his palm. For the first time, I wasn't writing him off as a drunk or a druggie.

"You could have something there."

I took a couple of shots of the mystery man.

"Stop taking photos. Shouldn't we help him? I think he was trying to tell you something."

I wasn't interested. I just wanted to get a few photos

and go. "You really want to do this? You don't know what you're getting yourself into."

Ceri was in full Good Samaritan mode.

"Look at him, John. He's hurt."

He was just a silhouette, swaying in the distance as the sun set bloodily on the horizon. The seascape was on fire behind him. I snapped away on continuous.

"Knock it off," Ceri said. "He needs our help."

She started making her way towards him.

"What's he doing here?"

I was still more interested in getting the photos. "The battery's a bit low," I said. "We should have charged it."

Ceri was getting impatient.

"Enough with the camera!"

We didn't reach the stumbling man. Two familiar figures beat us to it. Instinctively, we slipped behind the nearest statues and watched, out of sight.

"Look who's here. If it isn't the Gruesome Brothers."

The driver of the blue Lincoln was striding across the sand, followed by his companion. The passenger was stockier, his barrel chest straining at a leather jacket a size too small for him. I snapped the pair a few times and inspected the shots. I was still going through the photos when Ceri gripped my arm.

"They seem to know the walking man."

I turned absently.

"What did you say?"

She was pointing.

15

"The men from the car, Snakehead and Fat Lad, they know him."

That made me chuckle. "You've given them nicknames? Suits them."

I kept snapping away. I didn't share Ceri's concern for the staggerer.

"I'll get one or two with the flash."

Ceri didn't think that was a good idea.

"No, don't. They'll see us."

"You're not scared of Dumb and Dumber, are you?"

Just then, the wind gusted strongly, whipping sand in our faces. I leaned away, blinking. The wind dropped for a second and there was a loud *pop*. Simultaneously, the camera flashed.

"What was that noise?" I said.

"I don't know," Ceri said, "but I think you've upset them. They're heading straight for us."

She was right. To my surprise, they were running in our direction, Snakehead outpacing Fat Lad who was waddling, rather than running, blowing out his cheeks as he tried to keep up. There was no sign of the walking man.

"What's their beef?" I said. "All we did was take a photo."

They were still a good fifty metres away, but I wasn't planning to hang around to find out, so I set off towards the marina. Ceri scampered after me.

"What did you have to do that for, alert them to where we were?"

"I only took a photo. It's a free country."

"John, they look really mad about something."

"So what? They can't catch us. We've got too big a lead."

I didn't care how angry they were. They wanted some of me, did they? The moment I reached the dunes, I turned. They were even further behind now. Soon I was flipping our pursuers the finger with both hands. I danced up and down, yelling defiantly.

"Swivel on this, scumbags. You couldn't catch a cold, you sad morons. Look at you, Fat Lad." I blew out my cheeks. "Watch you don't have a heart attack."

I made loud, gasping noises and stuck out a stomach I didn't have then I dissolved into helpless laughter. Ceri gawped in horror.

"You're off your head, you are."

I was having too much fun. Ceri slapped at my hand.

"What's the matter with you? Let's go."

I was still jumping about on the sand, winding them up. "They don't scare me."

"Well, they scare the hell out of me," Ceri snapped. "You're crazy."

I finished my attempt at the haka.

"What, this crazy?" I turned my back on them and slapped my backside. "Come on, lads, kiss this."

We ran a bit further then turned. Ceri watched me for a moment then burst out laughing and joined in, taunting them.

"I'm no crazier than you, Ceri James. Go ahead, give them some stick."

Suddenly they were too close for comfort.

"Let's go."

Now that we'd had our fun, we raced off down the path, losing the men. We reached Marine Way and slowed our pace to a brisk walk. We slipped into an alley. We were only five minutes from home. Ceri still looked back from time to time. As the two men faded into the gloom, their shrinking forms posed no threat. Or so we thought.

"Do you want to come back to ours for a minute?" I asked.

"No, I'd better get back."

That's when her phone went. Maybe she had a boyfriend.

"Hi, Gemma."

Not a boyfriend, then. So far so good.

"Yes, I phoned you." She laughed. "No, some idiot bumped into me. Thanks for phoning back."

I watched Ceri talking on the phone and decided to make a call of my own. Mum answered on the third ring.

"I'll be back soon. We've just finished."

"Where are you, anyway?"

"Five minutes away. We've been getting pictures of the statues on the beach. I told you."

"Did you? Sorry, John. I'm run off my feet. Mind like a colander."

She wasn't kidding. Since Dad had gone abroad to work, she'd had a permanent harassed look.

"Anyway, I'll be home soon."

"No problem. I'll probably be gone by the time you get back. We're going out in a sec. It's Trinity's final rehearsal tonight."

I could hear my sister in the background, howling something about a leotard. Trinity's the ultimate drama queen. She's been doing gymnastics for years. She goes to the Lifestyles Centre on Park Road, a mile from where we used to live. There was some big competition in the offing so she was doing all the hours. Right now, she was throwing the mother of all hissy fits.

"Tell her to break a leg," I said.

Trinity was such a stress bunny. Mum whispered into the phone. "Break her neck is more like it if she doesn't calm down a bit." She called across the living room. "It's in your sports bag where you left it. Look, I've got to go, John. We're running late."

"Yes, see you . . ."

But she had already hung up.

". . . later . . ."

I found myself smiling. With my dad away in the Gulf, she had her hands full. I shoved the phone in my pocket. I was still thinking about the blue Lincoln and the confrontation on the beach when Ceri patted my arm.

"Something's bothering you," she said. "What gives?"

"I don't know. I've been thinking about what happened on the beach."

Ceri gave me a sideways look. "You're not still going on about the Gruesome Brothers, are you? It's over. Forget it."

19

"It's the way they reacted. All I did was take a photo. Don't you think it was a bit weird?"

Ceri obviously didn't think it was anything.

"You're overthinking it."

End of conversation. I offered to walk her home, but she gave me the cold shoulder.

"Your house is just here. There's no need to go out of your way for me."

"What if I want to?"

Her eyes searched mine.

"Look, I walk home by myself all the time. I don't need a bodyguard."

"I insist."

Ceri gave me a teasing look. "I thought you had homework."

Good memory, that girl.

"I do," I said. "Ten minutes walking you home won't make any difference."

Especially ten minutes in the company of a girl I fancied rotten.

We walked the streets in silence for the most part, exchanging the odd bit of small talk. We turned a corner and there was Greenways. It was a rambling residential house with a small, untidy garden.

"I'll see you tomorrow, then."

She barely even gave me a glance as she walked away.

"See you tomorrow."

It had started to rain. I turned my collar up against

the wind and the increasing downpour. That's when I saw something that had my heart slamming in my chest. There was a car turning the corner a hundred metres away. A blue Lincoln. With black alloy wheels. What the hell?

"Ceri!" I called. "The car."

She stared. When she didn't move, I grabbed her sleeve, bundled her over the nearest garden wall and crouched down. Ceri followed my lead.

"What makes you think it's the same one?" Ceri hissed.

She tried to pop her head up and I shoved her back down. She glared.

"Who are you shoving?"

"Ceri, it's the same car. How many Lincolns do you see on the street?"

"I'd never heard of a rotten Lincoln till just now." She shook her head. "It can't be them. You're paranoid."

"You think? How many flash American motors do you see on the street? It's not just the make. It's been modified, just like the one at the beach." I was talking fast, trying to get her to understand. "It's got alloys and vents. What are the chances of two cars with the same work done on them?"

This was mad. What was wrong with these people?

"Stay down," I ordered.

"Don't tell me what to do."

She was driving me mad, but I managed to force out the magic word.

"Please."

I stole a look over the wall, examined the guys in the

21

car and felt my blood turn to ice. "It's them all right, Snakehead and Fat Lad."

Ceri's eyes flashed fear. Now she was taking me seriously. "All this because we were cheeky? It doesn't make any sense."

A shadow stole over me. "It could."

"Meaning?"

"Think about it. What if there's something in those pictures? I said they were up to no good."

"Like what?"

"I don't know. Drugs?"

The car pulled up opposite the home.

"What are they doing?"

"They're parked outside the home, watching the street. They know we're here somewhere."

By now, Ceri's eyes were slashes of horror.

"So what's in the photos?"

An idea was forming, but I didn't want to go there. The rain was hammering from the sky, skipping off the pavements and leaving everywhere cold and slicked and shiny. Thunder grumbled out across the bay.

"Fat Lad's getting out."

The rain stopped as quickly as it started. The street was gleaming. Ceri was like a ghost, paler and more haunted than ever.

"What do we do now?"

"I don't know. He's going round the back. They definitely know we're here somewhere."

We felt exposed, crouching behind a wall just a few metres from the Lincoln.

"Look, if we stay put it's just a matter of time before they spot us. I say we get out of here."

"Where do we go?"

"Back to mine. We can go through the photos then I'll see you home later. They're not going to drive around all night, are they?" I took a deep breath. "OK, are you ready?"

"I hope you're not getting any funny ideas."

"Behave, will you? So, shall we go?"

Ceri nodded. "I don't have to be in early."

We crept along the wall to the gate. Snakehead was staring at the houses. Fat Lad was out of sight.

"On my count."

"What does that mean?"

I gave her a pitying look. Had she never watched an action movie?

"I count. On three we run and we don't stop. One, two, *three*."

We ran, ducking down, and crossed the road.

"Did they see us?"

"I don't think so."

Wishful thinking. They'd seen us.

I had my key in the door.

"Can't get used to this lock."

The door finally opened and we rushed in, as if demons had been chasing us. Ceri closed the front door behind her

23

and we both took a deep breath ... and laughed. Weird how you do that when you're scared.

Then she looked at me.

"So you haven't been here long?"

Maybe I hesitated, just for a moment, keen not to give anything away. I didn't want her asking any more questions. When I did speak, I tried to sound casual.

"No, we haven't been here long."

"Why did you move?"

Casual again. Forced casual.

"It wasn't my decision. My mum's from the north end. She wanted to be nearer her parents."

And that's all Ceri was getting. I wasn't about to share any family secrets with a stranger. She had nothing else to say so I led the way inside.

"Give me that memory card. If there is something on here, we need to know."

She looked around the house. I caught her eye. Had she never heard the phrase, curiosity killed the cat? For a moment I tried to see through her eyes and I made a note of every telltale sign of a family recently arrived: chests, cases, bags for life stuffed with belongings. We'd moved in the summer, but our life was still stored in boxes. I got my laptop, shrugged off my jacket and sat down. Ceri picked something up.

"You dropped this."

I took it from her absent-mindedly. It was a piece of paper folded in four.

"It's not mine."

"It fell out of your pocket."

"Are you sure?"

"I'm sure."

I set the piece of paper down on the table.

"Here, put the battery on charge, will you? There's a socket over there."

Ceri had to shove a packing case out of the way. I slipped my laptop from its case, turned it on, typed in my password and inserted the memory card in the slot.

"OK, what have we got here?"

I used the pad to move the cursor. Then the image appeared and I could feel my insides dissolving. Simultaneously, Ceri reacted as if she'd had an electric shock. Her hands flew to her face.

"Oh my God!" she gasped. "Is that real?"

"Of course it's real. We took it."

Suddenly it all made sense. That noise. It was a shot.

I scrolled through the next few frames. The rush of adrenalin was like a blast of hot air from a fan oven. We were looking at half a dozen photos of Snakehead, taken over a matter of seconds. He had his arm outstretched. I registered the definition of his muscular forearm. The images were as banal, as ordinary, as false-looking as they were shocking.

"The guy who bumped into you. They killed him. They murdered him."

"John, we've witnessed a murder."

I stared, numb with horror.

"What do we do?"

I snapped the laptop shut. "I don't know."

It was a few moments before I could reopen the computer and confront the image.

"Are we in danger?" Ceri asked, transfixed by what she had seen.

Stupid question.

She came to a decision and pulled out her phone. "I'm calling the police."

She paced up and down the living room, waiting for the operator to answer. When she got through, she put it on speaker so I could hear.

"Emergency – which service do you require?"

"Police."

Something made me remember the scrap of paper she'd handed me. I unfolded it and the horror turned into an impossible nightmare. It was as if somebody had reached a hand inside me and ripped my guts out. It wasn't possible. My thoughts raced. How? Then I saw Ceri with the phone in her hand. The conversation couldn't happen. I made a grab for it.

"John, what are you doing?"

"Give me the phone."

She stared.

"Give me the bloody phone!"

Then we were struggling.

"Have you gone crazy? I'm through to the operator."

I grabbed at her arm and the phone flew out of her hand.

"What's the matter with you?"

When she tried to recover her phone I pulled her back.

"Get off me. You've got a screw loose. I . . ."

She broke off, her voice cracking. A cold, dark blast of adrenalin hit me as I followed the direction of her stare and saw the car driving towards my front door. How the hell did they find us? Ceri was reeling with shock. The sight of the Lincoln tore the words out of her mouth.

"Get away from the window now!"

The world seemed to pitch and blur. Everything that had been solid and predictable collapsed like a fence in a storm. First the incident on the beach, then the picture, the note . . . now this.

"Kill the light."

From wherever the phone had landed, I could hear the operator's voice crackling out of the phone.

"Are you there, caller?"

I stared in disbelief at the Lincoln parked outside then I pulled Ceri back. She fell against me, but this time there wasn't a murmur of protest. We both had eyes on the car.

"What the . . .?"

I had her breath on my cheek and I wasn't thinking about anything but the danger outside. Blue bodywork. Black alloys. Vents. Fear was on my tongue like vomit.

"Oh my God!"

The headlights dimmed. Fat Lad got out, squinting as he read the house numbers.

"How did they get the address? Are these guys supernatural or something?"

Suddenly there was a ghostly pair of eyes floating down the street, peering into every window. Nowhere was safe. The Gruesome Brothers were already making their way over. I had time to register a few extra details. Snakehead was wearing cowboy boots with turned up toes and metal caps. Fat Lad walked with his feet splayed at angles like an oversized penguin. It was like something out of a movie, but it was real, horribly so.

"They're coming this way."

Finally, I knew what to do. "Ceri, we've got to bail. We're getting out."

"Where do we go?"

"I don't know." I pointed in the direction of the uglies. "Maybe you want to hang around and talk to them."

I shoved my laptop in its case, grabbed the camera and battery. A myriad of doubts and questions were racing through my mind. Nothing made sense. Those two men outside, they knew things that just could not be known. They were inhuman, like hounds sent from hell. Spotting us and following us to the street where Ceri lived was one thing. Tracking us here was something else. And what about the note? That was the clincher. Ceri knew nothing about it and I wasn't in a hurry to tell her. We had entered a twilight world where nobody played by the normal rules any more. The doorbell rang. I stuffed my things into a bag and bundled Ceri through the back door and locked it behind me.

"We've got to go." I made the shape of a gun with my thumb and fingers. "They popped that guy as cool as anything. These men are gangsters, Ceri. They're the real deal . . . and we're witnesses to a murder."

Her face was wild with fright. I led the way to the garden gate, flipped the catch and slipped out into the alley behind the house.

"Which way?" Ceri asked, stumbling along in my wake.

"You tell me. They could come from either direction."

"Listen."

Somebody was pounding on the front door. The sound rumbled through the house. A few doors away, a dog started barking. A figure appeared at the top of the alley, silhouetted in the light of a street lamp. We flattened ourselves against the bricks, waiting for him to go, and did an about-turn, staying close to the wall.

"Was that one of them?"

"I don't know. I'm not taking any chances." I grabbed her hand. "We need to put some distance between us and those men. We'll work out what to do the moment we feel safe."

I had Ceri's hand in mine. In the middle of all that madness, I had time to like the way she was hanging on to me.

"When do we feel safe? They find us wherever we go, whatever we do."

I didn't offer an answer. All I could say was: "This way."

"Where are we going?"

I turned and flipped on her. "You think I've got all the answers? Do you really want to hang around? Let's go."

There were no more words.

We ran.

Here's something I never realised until that moment. Life isn't like the movies. There's only so far you can run before your legs are like lead and you want to throw up. Fear makes it harder. You don't think. You just run. As far from danger as you can get. Within a few streets, my chest was heaving and I was dragging my feet. I bent double, hands on my thighs. My lungs were bursting. Opposite me, Ceri was leaning against a wall, gulping down lungfuls of air as if they were the last breaths she would ever take.

"Where are we going?" she asked.

"No idea," I wheezed. "Just away from them."

"Do you think they're still following?"

I shook my head, trying to get my breath back. "You tell me."

My gaze travelled through the gathering dusk. No sign of them.

"We can't go back to yours, John. Or mine. They know where we live, both of us. This sucks." She thought of something. "I left my phone in the house." She fixed me with a stare. "What got into you anyway?"

When I didn't answer, she continued.

"You've got yours. Call 999."

She saw me hesitate.

"I'm phoning Mum."

"Your mum. What are you, three years old? We need the police."

I gave her a reason. It wasn't the real one. "She needs to know they've been to the house. What if she arrives home and she finds those two on the doorstep?"

That kept Ceri quiet for the time being. The call rang out.

"Nothing," I grunted. "They must be in the gym. She turns her phone off when Trinity's on the apparatus. No distractions. I'll send a text."

Before Ceri could start harassing me again to phone the police, I dragged her back. The Lincoln was crossing the junction just up the road, going real slow, like kerb-crawlers. We had only gone a few streets and they had transport. They were cruising around, trying to spot us. If you've ever tried to make yourself invisible, you'll know what happens. You feel enormous. You feel so conspicuous, your skin crawls. There were trees on this street and we were a long way from the nearest street lamp, but I felt as if they had to have seen us. The car rolled on out of sight.

"They're not going to give up," I whispered.

Ceri's voice shuddered out, thin and vulnerable.

"I know. Oh God, I know."

We were both staring at the spot where we'd just seen the car.

"Which way?" I murmured.

Ceri shook her head. She was so scared, there were no words. She was choking on her own fear.

"OK," I said. "I know what to do."

It suddenly seemed so obvious. Our pursuers had a car. We were on foot. We needed an equaliser. There was only one place to go. I made a grab for Ceri's hand.

"The station."

She dug in her heels. "Why?"

I pulled and her shoes skidded on the pavement. Home was a few streets to our right, Ceri's a few streets in the opposite direction. We were on a quiet, tree-lined avenue, trying to stay out of sight.

"John, why the station?"

"Why not?"

She threw her arms in the air. "That's not an answer!"

"You just said it yourself. They know where you live. They know where I live. Think it through. They're mobile. What's faster than a car? A train."

"Phone the police," she begged. "Do it right now."

"And what do we do until they come? They're not going to give up. We're sitting ducks hanging round here." I tossed her a bone. "We can phone once we're on the train."

She seemed half-convinced. I took advantage of her hesitation.

"Look, we're all on our own and we need to be anywhere else but here. The nearest station is Waterloo. Have you got a better idea?"

Ceri shook her head.

"So we take the train, even if we only go one stop. We get the hell away from them. Once we're on board, we can make the call." I thought of something. "You do have your pass?"

She stared at me as if I was treating her like a little kid. "What are you, my mum?"

Something weird had just happened. She seemed to gag on the word *mum*.

"Ceri, are you OK?'

She batted the question away with a wave of her hand.

"Like you care. Like anybody cares. OK, let's go to your stupid station."

Then she was stamping away. What happened there? I'd just stood on a land mine. We reached the station without any more scares. Waterloo is our local one, on the Northern line, ten minutes or so from home. Maybe we'd finally got lucky. We were on the southbound platform, looking left and right. There was that feeling again. We were so exposed. It was as if this giant novelty hand was hanging over us. Here they are. Here they are. Hey, Mr Gangster Men. I stared down the line, willing the train to come. Lights gleamed in the murk. Then there it was.

I urged it on, saying under my breath, "Come on. Come on."

Ceri was on the same wavelength. They could appear any moment.

"Who are these guys, some kind of super-gangsters? They can read our minds or something?"

An elderly couple moved to the front of the platform.

Nearly there.

Then there was the roar of an engine and running feet.

"They're coming!"

They were pounding towards us. The couple turned then twisted round to look at us. After that, everything was running in slow motion. The train pulled into the platform. We threw ourselves on board.

"The doors are open!" Ceri screamed. "Close the doors."

There were a few passengers already on the train. There was the elderly couple. Everybody was staring.

"Please. Close the doors!"

Ceri stuck her head out of the door, staring down the platform, searching for the driver or the guard.

"Don't let them on. Please!"

Then the door closed and the train started to move. Snakehead was pounding on the glass, trying to get his fingers into the crack between the doors. Then he stumbled and the world rushed and he was gone.

"Ceri," I said. "Just sit down. They can't catch us now."

Some of the passengers were still watching us. Ceri stared them out.

"You sure of that?"

"Sure I'm sure. Trains go faster. They don't have to stop at lights."

"Yes, they do."

"OK, they don't have to stop at many. Railway lines are straight and roads are . . ."

Words failed me. Ceri planted her hands on her hips.

"Roads are what?"

A word came. The wrong word.

"Wonky."

"Wonky?"

I don't know if it was nerves or just the madness of the situation, but we cracked up laughing. Finally, Ceri came and sat down. Some people got off at the next station and we were left alone except for a guy in a hi-vis jacket at the far end of the compartment. Ceri leaned in close as the train pulled out of the station.

"You said you'd phone the coppers."

"I will. Just let me think."

Ceri was looking at me as if I'd just grown an extra head.

"Think? What are you thinking about? We just saw some guy put a gun to a man's head. *They blew his brains out.*" She acted out the scene to concentrate my mind. "What's to think about?"

I came to a decision. "I'll try Mum again."

It sounded even more pathetic than the first time I said it. Ceri rolled her eyes.

"Right, ask Mummy what to do."

I reacted. "Look, I'm phoning to warn her about those two thugs. You think it's funny, two guys with guns turning up at my house?"

That put a stop to Ceri's protests. I made the call. No answer. They had to have finished at the gym, but Mum wouldn't pick up if she was driving. That gave Ceri her cue.

"Phone the police. Phone 999."

Not an option, Ceri. Not an option. If you knew ... I tapped my teeth with the phone. That drove her crazy. I could see what she was thinking. You're on a train, pursued by a pair of homicidal thugs and you're with a guy who won't phone the police.

"What are you doing?" she demanded, lips pinched with fury. "Why don't you make the call?"

I will never forget the look on her face when I put my phone away. I had my reasons. She would never understand.

"Listen, my mum's been through a lot."

All that did was get Ceri's back up.

"And we haven't?"

She did the phone signal gesture with her thumb and little finger. "Phone – the – bizzies."

It was getting impossible to go on stalling, but how could I even begin to tell her the truth?

"I can't. There's stuff you don't know."

There was a look of disbelief all over her face.

"What stuff? We saw a *murder!*" She slapped her palms on my chest and gave me a shove. Tears were starting in

36

her eyes. She pounded her hands on me again. "What the hell is wrong with you?"

She made her hand into a gun and stabbed the barrel into my forehead. "A guy . . ." pause ". . . put a gun . . ." longer pause ". . . to another guy's head . . . bang."

She watched my face for a moment then made a grab for my pocket. We started wrestling for control of the phone.

"You don't understand."

I was strong enough to keep hold of the phone and push Ceri away. She looked utterly bewildered.

"So we do nothing? A guy gets killed and we just walk on by? Nothing to see here, folks."

High-vis jacket guy looked up from his paper.

"Keep your voice down," I hissed.

"Here's the thing," Ceri said. "Either you make the call or I walk down the train and ask that guy if I can use his phone."

I ached to explain, to show her the note Natty Dread had shoved in my jacket pocket, but it just wasn't possible. How do you betray your dad to a stranger? "Just give me a few minutes, will you? The priority is to warn Mum about those lunatics. What if she arrives home and they're waiting?"

Ceri cut through my excuses like a knife slashing through cane.

"The best way to keep them safe is to call 999."

My voice limped out. "Just give me some time. Please."

37

Ceri looked away. "And until then?"

"We stay on the train as far as town. It'll be safer there. There will be people around. We hang around until I can talk to Mum. By that time, maybe it will be safe to go home. What are we talking, half an hour? Are you saying you can't spare me thirty minutes?"

"You're not going to listen to me."

Her voice was dull and resentful. I'd bullied her into submission and I felt bad about it, but I had to buy time.

Had to.

"So it's a deal?"

She didn't understand. She blanked me and stared out of the rain-dimpled window. I sank back in my seat and watched the city lights rush by. How could I tell her my own father had betrayed us?

"We're here."

Ceri kept her face to the window. Liverpool Central station didn't look much like a refuge. We walked towards the ticket barrier and the echoing concourse. Ceri had eyes on me, but I didn't react. The station was deserted except for a few people coming out of the convenience store and a couple getting money out of one of the cash machines while parallel texting. Ceri was still hanging back.

"What's wrong?"

She approached and spoke to me for the first time in twenty minutes.

"What if they're outside, waiting?"

"It isn't possible."

"How do you know?"

I turned to face her.

"OK, listen to me. One, they would have to guess the station where we got off. That's a seven to one chance."

"You know how many stops there are?"

"I had time to count. You weren't talking to me."

That brought the hard look back into her eyes.

"Two," I said, "even if they guessed right, there is no way they could get here as quick as the train."

"The train has to stop at stations."

"And a car has to stop at lights or risk getting pulled by the bizzies."

"John, they popped a guy. You think they're bothered about a traffic offence?"

That made some kind of sense.

"OK, I'll go with your logic. We get away from the station soon as."

We passed through the ticket barrier. I led the way left through the Bold Street exit.

"Do you know where you're going?"

I kept walking.

"Away from the station," I grunted. "Have you got a better plan?"

Ceri jabbed her fists into her jacket pockets. "Yes, what about the one I talked about earlier, the one I suggested over and over again, but Mr Deaf to Common Sense wouldn't listen? We call . . . the . . . police. Got a problem with the police?"

I gave her the dead eye. "Liverpool 8 born and bred. You know, I just might have."

Ceri sighed. "You're kidding, right? You mean the race thing? This isn't the nineteen seventies."

I treated Ceri to a pitying look. "You really think things have changed that much? Ever heard of Black Lives Matter?" I rammed the point home. "How many black coppers have you seen lately?"

"One."

"And how many coppers have you seen?"

Ceri waited a beat before answering.

"I'm not defending the police. We get coppers coming round the home. Some are OK, but there's one guy who treats us as if we're scum." Ceri watched a couple kissing in a doorway. "You've got to understand the kids at Greenways. Some of them have been in care for years. There are bound to be one or two with problems."

I let her talk. It kept her mind off me calling 999.

"The guy I'm talking about, he just thinks we were born bad."

"Is that what he says?"

Ceri ignored me. "Some people look at kids in care and they see trouble. That's the way it is."

I tried a playful nudge. "Finished?"

That made her angry. "What, you can come over all badly done to, but the moment I do, I'm going off on one?"

40

She growled under her breath at not being taken seriously.

It was time to move the conversation on. "Are you hungry?" I fished in my pockets. "I'll stand you something to eat."

Ceri found a smile from somewhere. "There's a Wok and Go."

We wandered the streets around Liverpool's clubland, eating our food from the carton. From time to time, one of us would glance back, looking for some sign of our pursuers. There was no more talk of calling the police. She'd accepted defeat on that one.

It had turned into a fine night after the rain and there was moonlight on the damp streets. We got as far as the bombed-out church. A street cleaner wandered by with his cart. Two women stood smoking in a doorway opposite. Otherwise, it was all quiet on the western front. I tried Mum.

Still nothing.

My stomach twisted. This wasn't good. This was about Dad. Had to be. What had he done now? What the hell had he done?

"She'd better pick up soon," I said. "I'm nearly out of battery." I brandished the handset. "This is our lifeline and the charger's in my room."

The damp meant there was nowhere to sit down so we leaned against the wall and finished our noodles. Chinatown was a hazy blur in the murk. I binned the carton and turned the camera on. I flicked through the pictures.

"There's plenty for the coppers to go on here. I got the car reg, and look at this, you can see both men's faces clearly."

Ceri shivered. "How could this happen? I mean, we just went to get a few photos for our project."

"Bad things happen to good people."

Ceri seemed to hear something in my words. "Are you talking from experience?"

"Maybe I am."

"Would you care to elaborate?"

I sucked a morsel of food from my teeth. "No. You've got your secrets. I've got mine."

Ceri watched me make another call. Finally, somebody picked up.

"Mum?"

"John, where are you?"

Her voice sounded higher-pitched than usual, kind of brittle. She struck a false note and my skin prickled with unease. Ceri was staring.

"What's wrong?" she demanded.

I turned away, but Ceri walked in front of me, asking questions with her eyes. I mouthed the words: *somebody's there.*

"Mum, who's that in the background? Who's in the house with you?"

I already knew the answer. There was a burst of

crackling and interference, as if somebody was making a grab for the phone. There were the sounds of a struggle.

"Mum!"

There was more noise, a scream then Mum yelling into the phone. "John, don't come back here. Stay away. You know where to go . . ."

A man's voice broke in.

"If you know what's good for you, you'll do as I say. Your bitch of a mother doesn't call the shots." There was an adrenalin rush down my spine. He was still talking. "We've got your mother and your sister. If you want to see them again, you'll do exactly as I say."

There was more noise, a roar of fear and struggle. There was the man's voice again as he tried to stop Mum speaking.

"Give me that phone."

Now there was nothing but a barrage of sound.

"Mum!"

Finally, the phone cut out.

"It's them. They're in my house." I started to walk. "I'm going back."

Ceri blocked the way. Her eyes were desperate. "John, no. You can't."

She didn't understand.

"That's my mum, my sister." I beat my chest each time. "I have to go to them."

Ceri wouldn't budge. "Talk to me, John. You can't walk through me."

43

"Ceri . . ."

I was about to see a different side to Ceri James. She planted her feet.

"Go on, tough guy, what are you going to do against a pair of thugs like them? Killers. Last time I looked, you didn't have superpowers." She had my attention. "Two guys, John, two armed, ruthless gangsters. You need to think. The only thing that's going to stop those men is this." Ceri grabbed the camera and waved it in front of my face. "This is proof, John. Proof. It's our bargaining counter."

She finally had my attention.

"If you go running home, they get this. What do you think they're going to do, say thank you and let things go back to normal?"

"They're going to hurt my family."

"If they get hold of this memory card, there's nothing to stop them going one step further." She thumped my chest. "They can kill you." She pounded her own. "They can kill me. They can do us all in if they like." She found the image of the execution. "Look at it, John. Look at it! Do you think I'm joking? Really?"

I went a few metres, scrubbing at my scalp with my fingernails.

"Well?"

"Let me think."

Ceri shook her head. "The way it seems to me, you've done nothing but think."

She had a way of getting under my skin. "Meaning?"

44

She threw out her arms. "We're in the middle of Liverpool. It's getting late. What are we doing here?"

"Those men are in my house." I jabbed my finger. "They're in my home."

Ceri was wrong-footed for a moment. Then she returned to her mantra. "Phone the police."

"I can't, not now. They could hurt my family."

She let out a cry of frustration. "That's all I hear from you, excuses!"

We were staring at each other, eyes hard with fright as much as anger. When you need to punch the world in the face, your best friend can be the easiest option. I tried calling home. There was more bad news.

"The line's dead."

"They probably pulled the cable out."

I slumped against the wall.

"Well," Ceri demanded, "now what? We've nowhere to go, nobody to talk to. If you won't call the police, what do we do?"

I shook my head. "I don't know."

Ceri heard the fear in my voice. She approached, her expression softening. She closed her hand over mine.

"Don't jump to conclusions. That's what they want you to do. Maybe your mum's taken your sister somewhere safe."

"She would have phoned me back."

Ceri leaned her forehead against mine. Her breath was on my face.

"Don't make this hard, John. I'm trying to help. You want the truth? Maybe they can't call. Maybe . . ." She took a deep breath. "Look, we just don't know. There's nothing we can do."

"This is my family we're talking about."

Ceri still had my hands. "Listen to me. Please listen. Your family is safe. I know it. Those men wouldn't do anything. Not when we've got proof of what they did. Hand yourself over and those men are in complete control."

"I don't know . . ."

Pleading, hazel eyes fought for my attention.

"Yes, yes you do. It wouldn't make any sense. They're not in a position of strength, John." She glanced left and right, checking nobody was eavesdropping. "They can make all the threats they like, but we've got the murder on camera. We've got their faces."

I stared at my phone. "What do I do?"

"You calm down, that's what you do. You think. You're no good to your family if you fall apart. Yes?"

I slowly got on top of my emotions. "I suppose."

"Oh, say yes, for God's sake!"

"Fine. Yes."

"Right, we can't do anything for your mum and your sister, not now, not yet, but we can stay safe and we can keep this memory card away from those morons. That's our best shot. Yes?"

There was a moment's silence.

"John, talk to me."

"Yes." I allowed myself an uncertain smile. "When did you get so wise?"

"I didn't get wise. I got crazy. Those men made me crazy when they offed that guy right in front of me and I didn't even know what had happened. How did we not realise? When I think of that noise . . ."

I relived the loud pop. That's how men die, with a sound like a punctured balloon. There was a longer silence then Ceri spoke again.

"Thing is, I'm scared right now and I'm pretty much alone except for you. The only people I know are back at Greenways and, you know what, I'm in no hurry to go back. So if there's an alternative, tell me."

My mind was working overtime.

"John, if it's left up to me, we'll end up sleeping in a shop doorway and getting peed on by drunks. Now that isn't my idea of a fun night out, so over to you, my knight in shining armour. Let's hear how we stay out of the gutter."

Suddenly, to my surprise, she burst out laughing.

"What, you think this is funny?"

"No," Ceri said. "I don't think it's funny. Honestly, I don't. It was your expression, that's all. It was priceless. If you're not going to phone the police, we're on the streets."

"How can I phone the police? They've got my mum and sister."

That might have washed earlier. I remember the way Ceri was scared and clinging to me for support. Now she was angry with me.

"Keep telling yourself that," she said. "It's a load of rubbish. You were reluctant to call them way before that." She let her arms flop at her sides. "There's something going on here that I don't understand." She watched me, waiting for an explanation. None was forthcoming. "OK, shop doorway it is."

That's when I remembered what Mum said.

You know where to go.

"Hold on, I might know where I can get help. There's this mate of mine. His whole family is sound. That's what Mum meant."

"Has he got a name, this mate of yours?"

"Jimmy Addo. I'll make a call," I told her, holding up my phone. The battery level was low. "It could be the last one I'll get out of this thing tonight."

Jimmy said to meet him on the corner of Mulgrave Street and Upper Parliament Street. It would be my first return to Parly since we moved. It was a twenty-minute walk through the drizzle. Ceri was still angry over the phone calls. The only sound was the hiss of tyres on the rain-dampened streets and our own footsteps on the pavement. When you know somebody can come round the corner any minute with a loaded gun, a few echoing footsteps can feel like the pulse of blood in your brain. Ceri's eyes were everywhere. I had a feeling she had never been south of the city centre.

"Are we anywhere near Speke Hall?" she asked,

breaking the uncomfortable silence. "We had a school trip there once."

It made me laugh.

"Geography's not your strong point, is it? You're way off. Speke Hall must be, what, eight miles away, by the airport."

Ceri frowned.

"OK, so I'm a few miles out."

We turned left on Parly and there was the familiar figure of Jimmy Addo. I jogged over to the opposite pavement.

"Jimmy, hey Jim."

Jimmy shoved himself off the railings and came over. He had his hand outstretched.

"You found your way back then?"

"I haven't been gone long."

"It's months."

"Aw, did you miss me?" I bumped Jimmy's shoulder with my fist. "I thought we were planning to meet up. Remember that?"

"It was on my to-do list."

"Yes, whatever. Forgotten me so soon?"

I was pulling his chain. In a world that had gone nuts, Jimmy was somebody I could trust.

"So the trouble I mentioned, any ideas?"

Jimmy was about to answer when Ceri drew his gaze.

"She with you?"

That's embarrassing, I thought. Ceri had slipped my

mind completely. I took a step to one side, stretching out a hand.

"Oh yes, this is Ceri."

Jimmy raised an eyebrow.

"So is she your . . .?"

"I'm not his anything," Ceri objected, "and don't talk about me as if I'm not here."

"Does Ceri . . ." Jimmy made a hasty correction. "Do you have a second name?"

"James. I'm Ceri James."

Jimmy tugged at my sleeve then scrubbed quizzically at his scalp.

"This changes things."

"What do you mean?"

"There's a bed, lad. Bed. Singular." He gave a slight twitch of the head.

There was an uncomfortable silence.

"This trouble," Jimmy said, "you're both part of it then?"

"Yes."

"Are you going to tell me what kind of trouble?"

Not in front of Ceri, I wasn't. Jimmy knew about that other stuff, stuff I didn't want her knowing. I didn't want Jimmy letting something slip. I'd have to wait until she was out of the way.

"Later. I'd like to get off the street. The night has eyes."

At that, Jimmy gave the street a once-over.

"That bad?"

"Lad, it's mental." An image of Mum and Trinity in

a bare cellar crossed my mind. You know the scene. Unshaded light bulb. Bound wrists. Yes, I've seen all the *Taken* films and there's no way my mum can shin up a steel pole to get free. "Think the worst that can happen and add some."

Jimmy nodded and started to walk. I kept pace with him, while Ceri maintained a slight distance, what might be called a meaningful distance. Everything about Ceri was meaningful. Jimmy explained the situation.

"I told my dad. He's the one who sorted you a bed for the night."

Otis. Jimmy's dad. I'd known him all my life. Otis was the fixer, a serious-looking guy with a slab of a face and hair greying at his temples. Otis owned a few convenience stores and a café, knew some of the local councillors and had ideas about making Liverpool 8 a business hub. It seemed to mean making a shedload of money. Otis was the only guy I ever knew who ever had much disposable income to his name. He wanted out of Generation Brassic.

"Of course it's OK. Mum said you'd sort things for us."

"He's just done up the flat over the café with a view to renting it," Jimmy said. "I've got the keys." He glanced at Ceri. "Of course, he doesn't know about . . . *her*."

Ceri nibbled at her lip before raising another protest. "I thought I told you not to talk about me as if I wasn't here."

Jimmy held up his hands and made a big show of looking around.

"Anybody else you haven't mentioned?"

I shook my head.

"No, just Ceri. She's more than enough. I'd rather drag a bag of cats round town than spend an evening with this one."

Ceri gave my ankle a kick, overdid it and sent me stumbling across the pavement. Jimmy roared with appreciative laughter. I gave Ceri a wounded look. She held up a hand by way of apology and saw Jimmy watching. The café was a few minutes walk down Lodge Lane. Jimmy jangled the set of keys. That was the moment the madness started to reach another level. We really were on the run.

"The Yale is for the outside door. The black fob is for the flat." He finished his explanation. "The Chubb is if you come in the back way."

He led the way upstairs and buzzed his way in. There was a smell of paint and sawdust, but the flat was modern-looking, clean and tastefully furnished with a black three-piece suite, a TV in a black cabinet and pictures of the Mersey in black frames.

"Something tells me Otis likes the black and white look."

"It's mini-me or something."

I helped him out. "Minimalist."

"Yes, that."

I watched Ceri walking round the flat.

"How many bedrooms?" she asked.

"One."

"Beds?"

Jimmy shot me a glance.

"One."

"That's sorted then," Ceri said. "I get the bedroom. This bag of cats likes to be comfortable." She pointed at me. "You're dossing down on the settee."

Jimmy flicked my forehead.

"The lady's got your number, Romeo. I'll see if there are any spare blankets."

With Jimmy out of the room, Ceri flew at me.

"You didn't mention me!"

"We needed something fast. You were a complication I didn't need."

"Complication! It's like I don't even exist. Look you, we're in this together or I walk straight into the nearest police station."

"Sorry, I've got stuff on my mind."

Ceri backtracked.

"Right. Your mum and sister. I get it. Look, we're both stressed out. When are you going to tell Jimmy about . . . *the thing*?"

The thing.

She couldn't even bring herself to say the killing.

Jimmy was standing in the bedroom doorway.

"That's what I was about to ask. My dad wants to know what you've got yourself into."

"We didn't get ourselves into anything." I remembered the note Natty Dread shoved in my pocket. "It's going to take time to explain."

Jimmy tossed some bedding my way and leaned against the doorjamb. "Have you eaten?"

"A tub of noodles in town."

"So I'm guessing you're still hungry."

"Starving. You?"

Ceri nodded. "Ditto."

Jimmy glanced at the wall clock, also framed in black.

"The chippy will still be open. I'll get you something then you can brief me."

Ceri came out of the bathroom.

"Jimmy's pretty thoughtful," she said. "He brought toothpaste and brushes."

Thoughtful? She didn't know the half of it. Jimmy's whole family was pure gold. Even when Otis's marriage broke up, he was always there for us. The Addos had been that way my whole life. Without them, I don't know where Dad would be now. When he wouldn't listen to his own mum and dad, he listened to Otis, though it took a while. I couldn't even hint at any of this to Ceri. Instead, I muttered something non-committal.

"Yes, he's like that."

Ceri looked around. "Where is he?"

"He just left."

I was lying on the settee, staring at the ceiling, wondering where my mum and sister were at that moment. I was back in the room with its bare light bulb. The whole thing gave me a sick feeling, thinking what might have happened to them, but what was I supposed to do other than have nightmares? Otis was in touch with Dad. I just had to wait. Ceri dropped into the armchair opposite. There was rain on the window. It made the world outside look alien and strange, a realm of blurs and bubbles.

"So how did he take it, the shooting and all?"

I crossed my ankles. Jimmy had listened to my story without saying a word, just the odd whistle between his teeth.

"He took it. They're that kind of people, Jimmy's family. They cope with things. Otis is going to swing past our house to see what's happening."

Ceri leaned forward. She started picking at her nails. "Right." She padded across to the window and closed the blinds. "What now?"

"Otis says he'll be round when he knows something."

"So no news is good news?"

I was doing my best to sound upbeat.

"Is right."

I sat up. "I don't know how I'm going to sleep tonight. That photo keeps going through my mind. That threatening voice down the phone, Mum yelling, it's too much to handle." I stared at my phone. "Why doesn't somebody ring? I'm going crazy here."

Ceri dropped her head forward, coppery hair tumbling over her face.

"Same here," she mumbled through the curtain of hair.

"I just want this to end. If you won't go to the police then we're in limbo."

"Ceri, I can't. I need you to trust me."

"How does that work? I don't even know you."

That was true. I did my best puppy eyes.

"Please."

She didn't argue. I made an observation. "You've calmed down a bit."

"You think I'm calm?"

She held out her right hand as if to show that it was trembling. I couldn't see anything.

"Resigned is what I am. Nobody cares what happens to me anyway."

"What about the people at the home?"

"Taking care of me is their job. There are different people all the time. It's not like having somebody who loves you."

"There's got to be somebody."

"Yes, my nan, but she's too ill to do anything." She was still playing with her hair. "It's so unfair. Why do good people get ill?"

That's when I made my announcement. "Jimmy didn't just sort food." I produced the bottle of wine. "He thought we might need a nightcap, you know, keep the nightmares at bay."

Ceri lifted the curtain of hair and fixed me with her hazel eyes. I got a tight feeling in my throat when she did that.

"That's if you drink."

"Neither of us is supposed to drink. We're underage."

I gave her a pitying look. "Since when did that stop anybody?"

Ceri met that with a smile. "Do you . . . drink, I mean?"

"I'll give it a go if you will." I offered her the bottle. "So, are you up for it?"

"Why not? I'm going to get off my face. Bottle opener?"

I found one in the kitchen.

"That Otis, eh? All mod cons."

I removed the cork and took a swig. It turned out wine wasn't all it was cracked up to be. Maybe you just ignore the taste to get the effect.

"That bad?" Ceri asked.

"It's like vinegar."

I handed the bottle over.

"If it does the job and conks us out, who cares? I don't want a sleepless night seeing the gun at that guy's head. I'm getting rat-arsed."

Ceri took a swig.

"Here's to staying safe." Then she thought of something. "How did Jimmy get served in the offie? He looks younger than we do."

"He didn't. This is Otis's vino. Didn't you see the wine rack in the kitchen? He has it on show to impress prospective tenants."

Ceri handed over the bottle.

"Are you still thinking about your family?"

She couldn't imagine. The idea that I was here, warm and safe in this flat while they were . . . anywhere, it made my skin crawl. Still does to this day. All that darkness.

"What can I do? Can't call anyway. The battery's all but dead. Jimmy says he'll bring a charger round in the morning on his way to school. We've got to sit tight."

"You trust Otis that much?"

I necked the wine then wiped my lips.

"Listen, Jimmy and me, we go back a lifetime. OK, sixteen years isn't much of a lifetime, but we're brothers, get me? We look out for one another. His family is my family. My family is his."

Ceri took the bottle back.

"That must be nice."

"It is." I'd picked up on the sadness in Ceri's voice. "So your gran's ill?"

"Yes, the big C. Breast cancer."

"I'm sorry."

"I was supposed to go and see her tomorrow. She's had an op." She gave a deep sigh. "I don't even know what kind of state she's in."

"What about your mum?"

Ceri looked away. Her voice rasped angrily. "That bitch? She dumped me like I was nothing. She left me with my nan and walked away. My dad cleared off when I was a baby. Looks like everybody in my life leaves me or dies."

Ceri took a long gulp as if she was trying to wash the

poison out of her life then she thrust the bottle back my way.

"Look," I said, "you can't call your mum a bitch, no matter what she's done."

"Can't I?" Ceri snapped. "She's a rotten, lousy, selfish bitch. There, I just did it again. Do you want to make something of it?" She chewed on her bottom lip. "Look, I don't want to have this conversation. My nan is all I've got and she's going to die." She sighed heavily.

I did my best to be helpful. "You don't know she's going to die. They can treat cancer, you know. Most people survive it these days."

Ceri eyeballed me. "Is that right, Doctor John? Well, thanks for the consultation, but no thanks." She scowled. "Piece of advice. Pass that bottle and keep your trap shut."

I'm not the kind of guy who can keep his mouth shut for long. For the next hour we drank and we talked, then we drank some more, but we didn't talk family.

Family was out of bounds.

It was mostly about Ceri. She talked. I listened, which was a novelty for me. She kept coming back to this friend of hers.

"She special then, this Gemma?"

"It's crap going into care, but my nan was too ill and my mum was too useless and off her head. Gemma was like a big sister. She looked out for me."

"But she's not at the home now?"

Ceri shook her head.

"She got too old so they cut her loose."

"What, dumped her on the street?"

Ceri took a swallow of wine and grimaced.

"No, she got a flat, on the North Park estate, but she couldn't work the washing machine or anything. Her benefits got sanctioned. She's always brassic. It's not right. She's dead pretty, but her clothes are always dirty and her hair's a mess."

"Surely, there's somebody to give her advice."

Ceri looked at me as if I had just crawled out of the toilet.

"Only somebody with a mum and dad could say that."

I thought about arguing back, but in the end I kept my thoughts to myself. Sometimes having parents is as hard as having none. Ceri didn't know what I was thinking.

"She's got nobody. One minute she was a kid. Next thing she knows she's got to do everything herself. She can't cope. I should give her a call."

She looked hopefully at the phone on the wall. "Is that working?"

"No, it isn't connected. I checked."

Can I use your laptop? She does Facebook on her phone."

"Facebook's an open space, isn't it? You don't know who's reading your posts. What security settings has she got?"

"I don't know."

"Then best not."

It was a long time before I got to sleep. It was that image. The cellar. The light bulb. Mum and Trinity scared and alone. So I did it. I texted Dad. The message was simple.

How could you?

You promised.

Then the battery gave up the ghost. Dead. I could have charged my phone through the laptop, but I didn't have a cable.

So it was Ceri, me and the darkness.

I woke suddenly the next morning. Somebody was ringing the doorbell. I pinched at my eyes and staggered over to the window in my boxers. Jimmy was standing in the street, shouting up at the window.

"Hey, Sleeping Beauty, are you deaf or something? How long does it take to crawl out of your pit, Rip Van Stinkle?"

I pushed the window further open.

"Why don't you invite the whole street to come and listen?" I dropped my voice, to a volume where even Jimmy would struggle to hear. It was a subtle hint that he needed to zip it. "I'll come down."

I squirmed into my trousers and listened at the bedroom door. Satisfied that Ceri was still asleep, I stumbled downstairs on my bare feet, bouncing off the wall, I was that tired. The pile was thick. In uncomfortable times, it made me feel comfortable. Otis was a man who knew his furnishings. Jimmy stepped into the hall. A familiar figure followed him inside and closed the door behind him.

Otis.

"Any news?"

"The guy that got offed, he's known."

"Known?"

"What have you got yourself into, John?" Otis asked.

"I'm not my dad," I told him. "None of this is down to me, Ote." I let it sink in. "So the murder victim, who is he?"

"He's got history, lad. Did you ever hear the name Leroy Brown?"

"No." Then something moved at the back of my mind. "Maybe."

"You should. We were at school together. He was round your house a few times."

That made my skin crawl. I still had the piece of paper in my jacket pocket. Dad knew the victim.

Jimmy chipped in.

"This is heavy. What have you got yourself into?"

I shoved my hands under my armpits and watched the street.

"What time is it?"

"Half eight. I've got to get a move on." Jimmy thrust a carrier bag at me. "There's a change of clothes for you and Ceri."

"Open a boutique, did you?"

Jimmy laughed. "I raided my sister's wardrobe. They look about the same size." A brown paper bag followed. "Breakfast."

I stuck my nose in the bag. The contents smelled good and looked bad. Crushed is what these brioches were.

"What are these?"

"Chocolate brioches."

"Come again?"

Otis explained. "They're French. We have them in the café."

Jimmy added his two pennyworth. "It makes the place ambient."

Otis corrected him. "It gives the place ambience."

"Yes, that too."

I turned my attention to Otis.

"Did you go to ours?'

Otis took a moment to answer.

"There's nobody there, lad. The lights were out. I had a nosey. I took a chance and knocked. Nothing." He saw the look on my face and hurried out a correction. "I looked through the window. There was no sign of a struggle. You know, nothing broken. Listen, I'm going to keep looking, put the word round some people in the know."

I wished we didn't know any people in the know. I thought about that note with Dad's details. That's what got all this crap started in the first place.

"The main thing is, you stay put here. We don't know what those guys are capable of."

I relived the scene on the beach. "That's the trouble, Ote. We do." As an afterthought, I said, "I texted Dad last night. Didn't say much."

I didn't elaborate, didn't say my phone was off so he couldn't get back to me. Why would I want to talk to Dad? This was down to him.

"I thought you were out of battery."

"There was enough juice for a text."

"Your old fella knows what's going down," Otis said. "I rang him in Doha. He's getting a flight back soon as. He'll get this sorted."

The past that wouldn't let go. I didn't tell Jimmy about the note. Maybe he already knew.

"Any luck finding me a charger?"

Otis handed it over.

"Listen to me and listen good, John. Don't do anything stupid. This will take careful handling. You don't want the Plod storming in with their number twelves."

"Is that what Dad thinks too?"

"We're agreed on this one. If they've got your mum and Trinity banged up somewhere, you don't want the coppers involved. It's going to take negotiations. Your dad'll sort it."

A wave of anger broke over me. "What, like he sorted it last time? And the time before that."

"One question," Otis said. "Do you trust him?"

I waited a beat. How do you answer something like that?

"I suppose."

"Then you sit tight and let him do his thing. There are only so many guys who could be behind this. He's arranged a few days' leave. He'll be home tomorrow if everything goes to plan. One day, John, you give him one day."

"Fine. I'll wait."

"And your lady friend?"

"Jimmy told you about Ceri then?"

"He told me. You like making things complicated, don't you?"

"Ceri stays out of the loop. This is on a need-to-know basis, and she doesn't."

Otis heard me out then he gestured to the bag.

"Oh, I forgot to say, there's an envelope inside. There's a wad of cash in case of trouble."

My heart slammed.

"Why would there be trouble? I thought we were safe here."

"Everything is sound. It's a precaution, is all. There's a couple of numbers written on it so you've got a lifeline if those guys find you."

I reacted. "You think that's possible?"

"Of course not, but you've got to be ready, just in case. Everybody needs a back up plan. If, by some miracle, they do show, use the money to get yourself somewhere and lay low."

They won't show.

If they do show.

He wasn't giving me much confidence.

"Your dad's back tomorrow so you only need to stay

below the radar for one day. Trust nobody. Any means necessary, right?"

So Otis thought I could survive on my wits. Flattering.

"Ote, I don't think I'll ever feel safe again."

"Chin up," Jimmy said. "You're not alone. We're all here for you, lad." He winked. "Let's face it, there's no chance the Gun Boy Two are going to come calling here. You're safe as houses."

I fist-bumped his shoulder. "Nice one."

"Later."

"Oh, if you need it, there's a back way out."

I watched them go, wishing he hadn't added that last bit. I shoved the front door shut, turned round and saw one that led into the yard. I glanced outside. It wasn't much of a yard, maybe a couple of metres square, but there was a gate. There was the low rumble of traffic out on Lodgie. I explored for a few moments, worked out a plan then made my way upstairs.

I listened at the bedroom door again. Ceri was still sleeping. I started breakfast and plated up the brioches. There was a coffee maker in the kitchen. I didn't have a clue how to work it. After some rummaging, I found an instruction booklet in a drawer. Otis was thorough. There was a noise and Ceri appeared. She looked dishevelled. Cutest kind of untidy I ever saw in my life. Ever since I'd started taking an interest in girls it had been *hubba, hubba, woof, woof,* physical attraction. I felt all that when I looked at Ceri, but a whole lot more besides that I didn't quite understand.

"Do you drink coffee?"

"Not usually, but it smells nice. I need something. I can still taste that wine from last night. Bleuurch. If that's drinking, you can keep it."

"You didn't enjoy it, then?"

"I'll never be an alchy, that's for sure. I'll heat up some milk. My nan used to make me milky coffee. It was all right."

Weird how she talked about her nan as if she was already dead. She flicked a curtain tassel. "Everything was all right when I was with my nan. She made me feel safe."

I took it personally.

"And I don't?"

She frowned me into silence. We sipped coffee and ate brioches.

"Where did the cakes come from?"

They were more like pasties with chocolate instead of meat.

"Otis has been round with Jimmy."

"Any news?"

"There's nobody at home, no sign of Mum or Trinity. Either they've gone into hiding like us, or . . ." A wave of hopelessness swept over me. I swallowed hard, the words choking in my throat. "Sorry."

Ceri rested a hand on my arm.

"You've no need to bottle it up. I don't buy all this boys-don't-cry stuff."

That did it. I fell apart, pawing the tears away.

"Whatever. I'm not crying in front of . . ."

"In front of a girl?"

"In front of anybody."

Ceri put the last morsel of brioche in her mouth, chewed, washed it down with milky coffee and put her question.

"Anything else?"

She saw the way I hesitated.

"John?"

"No, there's nothing."

"I don't believe you."

"There's nothing else, OK? Otis says we sit tight while he tries to get more information."

Ceri wasn't satisfied. She licked a fingertip to pick up a crumb and put it on her tongue.

"Why? If your mum and sister have been kidnapped, you go to the police. End of."

"My dad says different."

I felt the heat rush down my spine. Too much information.

"Come again?"

The cat was out of the bag. Big cat. Not much of a bag.

"John, what did you just say?"

"Otis has been in touch with my dad, OK? He's on his way back."

Ceri digested my reply, though it seemed to stick in her throat.

"I can understand your dad returning, but why would he want to keep the police out of it?"

"They've got Mum and Trinity! Isn't that reason enough?"

"Yes, and most men would have been on the blower by now. Something doesn't add up. John, you've flipped every time I've mentioned the police. What gives?"

There had to be a good answer, a convincing answer, but I couldn't think of one without mentioning the past and that was something I had no plans to do.

"That's not the way we do things."

"It's the way everybody does things. It's what the police are for. Come on, you've seen the movies. If there's a kidnap, the bad guys say don't go to the police." She caught my eye. "You know why they say that? Because it's exactly what they're afraid of."

I cut her dead.

"We're not going to the police!"

I was yelling. Ceri winced, making me cool it. She saw that I wasn't going to give a repeat performance and flopped against the back of the armchair.

"Give me one good reason why. I've had all night to think . . ."

"So the wine didn't conk you out?"

Ceri wasn't about to let me knock her off her stride.

"I didn't drink enough. No more interruptions, John. You're going to hear me out. I've had time to think. We should have phoned the coppers right away. It's understandable. We were scared. The world had gone crazy. Now that we've had a night's sleep . . ."

"I didn't sleep."

"Yes, you did. I heard you snoring."

"I don't snore."

She glared. "Are you going to let me finish?"

I folded my arms. "Fine, say your piece."

Ceri took a deep breath. "Now that we've had a night's sleep, we should be thinking clearly. If your mum and sister are in danger, we don't waste any more time. We go to the police."

No way, I thought. *It isn't going to happen.*

"You're out of your depth. You don't know what's going down here."

Ceri watched me, brow furrowed, eyes betraying both suspicion and disbelief at my reaction. Finally, she spoke.

"There's stuff you're not telling me. I heard you talking to Jimmy, but I couldn't make out the words. You owe me an explanation."

I dug my heels in. "There's nothing. I told you there was nothing."

"And I don't believe you!"

I buried my face in my hands and stayed that way for some time. How the hell was I going to get out of this? Eventually, I surfaced.

"You're right." My voice was low and defeated. "Yes, you're right. There is something else. The guy on the beach, my dad knew him."

It was as if the ceiling had fallen in on Ceri. I can't remember ever having seen such an expression of horror before.

"Look, I still feel muzzy after that wine and I need to gather my thoughts. I'm going to have a shower then we'll talk. Are you good with that?"

Ceri didn't say a word, but I took it as a yes. I picked up the charger and plugged it into the wall. The charging symbol appeared on the screen.

"Shower," I said. "Then we'll talk."

It was the longest shower of my life. I stood under the hot spray, face raised, wondering how to tell my story; no, correct that, Dad's story. It's as if I grew up with two dads. One was the caring, loving father who spent hours playing football or showing Trinity and me round the Liverpool waterfront. The other was this ghost dad who walked in shadows and had another life we knew nothing about.

The stuff he did back then is more myth than story, a legend formed of half-truths. I grew up in a world of rumour. There were fleeting figures, booming voices, moments of glaring brilliance as if a beam of light had torn through the murk of ignorance. I remember the quarrels, the darted glances, the echoes of a menace unspoken.

Finally, I squeezed off the jet of water and started to dry myself, wiping away a circle of condensation and staring at my reflection in the mirror. It was a face that seemed to have aged suddenly: eyes that brooded, lips pulled tight in anticipation of the confession to come. I rested my forehead against the mirror. It was time to face the music. I eased the door open a crack.

"Jimmy brought some clean clothes. Can you shove them through?"

There was no answer.

"Ceri, can you hand me my clothes?"

Still no answer. Alarm bells started ringing. I wrapped a towel round me and walked into the living room. She was gone. I checked the bedroom and kitchen. She was gone, all right.

"Ceri, you idiot!"

I scrubbed myself as dry as I could and scrambled into the clean clothes. I shot a quick glance out of the window, but there was no sign of her. I stumbled down the stairs and out of the door.

"Ceri!"

There was a woman passing.

"Have you seen a girl? She's got red hair."

A smile.

"Yes, she nearly knocked me over."

"Which way did she go?"

She pointed. I set off in the direction of Princes Park. This was all I needed. If Ceri went to the police, this whole thing could get even worse. Those men had my mother and sister and they weren't in the charity business. I reached the junction. I'd only just had a shower and I was clammy with sweat already. My shirt was sticking to my back. I swept the street with a glance: left, straight ahead, right. Then there she was, on the opposite side of the road, heading towards town.

"Ceri, hold up!"

She started to run, but not fast enough. I weaved through the traffic and pounded across the central reservation.

"Ceri, are you crazy? Come back. We need to talk."

I caught up with her halfway down Princes Avenue and made a grab for her. She turned to face me.

"Get away from me!"

"Ceri, be reasonable."

"Reasonable? Are you kidding? You've lied to me."

"I didn't lie."

"Did you tell me the truth?"

OK, time to take it on the chin.

"No."

She threw up her hands.

"That's it, I'm out."

She was walking again.

"Ceri, where do you think you're going?"

"Police station."

I called her bluff.

"You're going the wrong way. The nearest is Admiral Street."

She examined my face. All I saw was confusion.

"You don't want to go to the police, do you?"

She dissolved into tears.

"I don't know. I'm scared and alone and you won't tell me anything."

"I'm going to level with you. Promise."

Promise. That's what Dad said. No more crap. No more being afraid.

Promise. I was my father's son, all right. King of the liars.

"Look, we're not safe on the street. Let's go back."

Suddenly it was as if gunmen were coming from every direction. Ceri looked around and admitted defeat.

"I don't even know where I was going."

Back in the flat, I told my story the best way I could.

"That guy who died on the beach, he's got a name. Leroy Brown."

"Who was he?"

"Petty criminal. Not one of the main men."

"What's the connection with your dad?"

I shrugged.

"I don't know."

She reacted angrily.

"You said you'd tell me everything."

"I am. This Leroy guy was at school with Otis."

"Is that what this is about?"

"No, Otis steers clear of guys from his past."

"You sure about that?"

"I'm sure."

I produced the scrap of paper and handed it to her.

"What's this?"

"The connection."

She looked confused so I tapped the note.

"See this address? That's where I live. That's our phone number. That's my dad's mobile."

"This is why you wouldn't call the police?"

I nodded. "Right."

"I'm listening."

"There's a reason we moved," I began. "My dad's got a past."

Ceri scowled.

"I got that."

I let her words pass without comment. "He was in and out of trouble when he was about my age, you know. The family tried to talk him out of it, but he refused to listen."

"So what did he do?"

I hesitated.

"Nobody's ever told me the whole story, not in detail anyway. I've had to work it out for myself the best I could, but I've heard people talking."

Ceri fiddled with the gold band on her ring finger. She had mentioned her nan gave it to her on her fourteenth birthday.

"There's something you have to understand, John. If I'm going to go along with this madness any longer, you need to be completely open with me. I want to know what I've got myself into here. Are you saying your dad is some kind of gangster?"

"No. No way!"

Maybe I was protesting too much. He was in the company of hard men, so what did that make him?

"Look, he was young, stupid. He was on the fringes, a kid who got too close to the flame, but one day he saw something . . ."

"Like us, you mean, he was a witness?"

The word *witness* pulled me up short. It made a kind sense. That's what we shared, father and son. We were witnesses.

"Yes, right, a witness."

"What was it he saw? A murder?"

"No, nothing like that. A straightener."

Ceri frowned. "What's that?"

"You're kidding? You've never heard of a straightener?"

"No."

"It's like this. Two guys have a problem. They sort it with their fists. Last man standing wins."

"I think I was better off not knowing."

My thoughts drifted off to an overheard conversation. "The fight my dad saw was between two real warlords, guys who ran whole areas of the south end."

"Drugs?"

"I suppose. Other stuff too, knock-offs, contraband, loan sharks. They're responsible for half the crime in the city."

I thought of the man on the beach. Leroy Brown. Would he have been at the event?

"So these two men had a fight?"

I knew exactly how bad all this sounded.

"They did, but not just any fight. The stakes were high. If you get whipped, you're supposed to admit defeat and that's an end to it. The guy who was losing had other ideas. He had a knife concealed in his sock. He shanked his opponent."

"He stabbed him?"

"That's right, put him in the Royal on life support. He broke the rules."

Ceri had her hand over her mouth. She was quiet for a few moments then put another question.

"These two men, do they have names?"

Good try, Ceri, but you really don't want to know. We're talking men who bury guys in concrete for fun. "Everyone has a name," I grunted.

"But you're not saying?"

"You can have a nickname, if you like. The guy who came out on top, even if he cheated, they call him Magnum."

"Named after the gun?"

"The ice cream."

"Come again?"

"He's partial to ice cream. I'm not making it up."

Ceri seemed to be wondering if I was.

"Were these black guys or white guys?"

"Oh, here we go."

She stared at me.

"Is that your idea of a criminal?" I growled. "Black guy with a gun? Crime doesn't have a colour, just a price tag. Both gangs were white, if you really want to know. Dad was just junior muscle, a stupid kid who'd got in way over his head."

"That doesn't sound like you talking."

She was right.

"It's what Otis told me."

Ceri digested this. "Where does Leroy Brown come into all this?"

She had me there.

"I don't know," I told her. "The victim pulled through. Just. After that, it was all about vengeance. Suddenly everybody who had anything to do with that fight felt like a prisoner on Death Row, breathing a sigh of relief if they got through to the next day."

Ceri thought maybe she knew what was going on.

"Was it actually your dad who got into this fight?"

It was a reasonable assumption, but no, that wasn't it.

"I told you. He was a bystander."

"Right," Ceri scoffed, "bystander."

"OK, Dad could handle himself. Still can. Dad was Magnum's bodyguard."

"So not just a bit player?"

I conceded the point. "OK, I'll give you that, but the moment he saw that fight, the penny finally dropped. He was playing with the big boys and he didn't like the rules of the game. He wanted out of the life. Trouble is, there are men who won't let you walk away. Magnum was one of them. It's all about trust, and somebody who walks away can't be trusted. My mum flipped. She was going to throw Dad out of the house."

"But she didn't?"

"Oh, she did."

Ceri looked confused.

"She told him to sling his hook, but she relented and took him back a month later. Dad can charm the birds out of the trees. Somehow, through it all, I've always known my parents were for keeps. There was one condition. Dad had to stay clear of trouble and we had to save up enough money to move."

"That's how you ended up in Crosby?"

"Yes, eventually. Mum's from up this end."

I carried on. "Mum thought Dad would have less temptation if he moved up here, out of the old neighbourhood. He's been avoiding these people, but there are always rumours. There's somebody looking for him. The phone goes and nobody speaks. It isn't over. That's what made him take the Doha job, to get out of the country, out of harm's way. Otis arranged it."

"That's a surprise."

"Don't knock it. But for Otis, my dad would be in prison or dead."

"Dead?" Ceri said. "Do you really think so?"

"Somebody took out our front window with a bullet," I told her. "That real enough for you?"

Ceri just stared.

"The house you live in now?"

"No, our old house." I was stumbling through the story now. It was complicated and I didn't want her to know everything. "We got a phone call telling us to get out, or it could have been worse. The whole family was going crazy. Dad had shamed them."

"So you made a new start?"

"Tried to," I said. "Otis has got contacts all over. After the window went in, him and everybody tore into Dad for being so stupid. Nothing's happened in a while so we thought maybe he was finally safe."

"But he isn't?"

"Doesn't look like it. There's got to be a reason Leroy Brown came looking for Dad."

"But you don't know what it is?"

"No."

Ceri brooded over my story, thinking about the things I'd told her.

"So this is why we're on the run, because of you?"

I had just about enough pride left to raise a protest.

"How's it because of me?"

Ceri added a rider. "Because of who your father is."

We glared at each other then Ceri broke eye contact. "This is too much to get my head round. There's got to be more that you're not telling me."

There was plenty I wasn't telling her.

"I've told you what I know. Dad doesn't share. It's a

time in his life he doesn't want to discuss. Him and Mum, they've still got issues over it, him putting me and Trinity in danger. One time, she threw a cup at him."

"I hope it hit him," Ceri said.

"It smashed against the wall."

Ceri's face betrayed suspicion. "You're sure he's the only one involved in this mess?"

"Meaning?"

"Otis. He seems larger than life, somehow."

"No way."

"Sure?"

"Sure I'm sure. Otis is sound, true as steel. He says crime is a mug's game. Business is the way to go, legit business." I saw the way she looked at me. "What, you think I'd make up something like this?"

Ceri gave me a sidelong glance. "You haven't been doing too well telling me the truth so far. Maybe you don't know the truth."

There was an accusation in her voice.

"It's not an easy thing to admit," I said. "Anyway, the answer to your question is no, nobody else in our family has ever crossed the line. My grandparents are stand-up people. It nearly destroyed them when Dad went off the rails. He's a one-off."

"So what went wrong?"

I shot her a look that said *conversation over* and checked the progress on charging my phone.

"Are you going to try your mum again?" Ceri asked.

I stared at the screen, the battery symbol, the lightning-flash charging symbol.

"I don't know what to do. Otis said to sit tight."

"And you always do what Otis says."

"Meaning?"

"Don't you ever think for yourself?"

"It was thinking for myself got us this far," I retorted.

Ceri looked around the flat.

"Yes, holed up in a flat in Liverpool 8, waiting for a knock on the door from Tom and bloody Jerry."

"Well, you got one thing right," I said. "We're waiting for a knock on the door. So we wait, Ceri. We wait, because Otis is the man and he's going to see us right."

For want of anything else to say, Ceri examined her crumpled clothes.

"I'm going to get changed. How did Jimmy know my size?"

Because Jimmy spent a lot of time sizing up girls is why. "He's good at estimating girls' figures."

Ceri grimaced. "Why does that not surprise me?"

She took her new clothes into the bedroom. When she reappeared I gave a low whistle. She was quite something in the right gear.

"You can cut that out," she snapped. "Wolf whistling is sexist."

"It's a compliment," I said. "You look more like a girl."

Ouch, that wasn't wise. Ceri planted her hands on her hips.

"And what did I look like before?"

"A *school*girl."

"It didn't stop you staring."

True. She had me there. I'd been staring at Ceri since the first time I saw her.

A clock ticked. In the kitchen the fridge gave a shudder. Otherwise, the only sound was the odd car passing in the street outside.

"Feels a bit surreal, doesn't it?" Ceri said. "It's as if we fell through a hole in normal life."

"So which one of us is the white rabbit?"

She thought about it. "We both are."

I flipped open my laptop and stared at the image of the shooting. Ceri had a question.

"Have you got a wifi code?"

"Yes, it's written on the envelope."

Ceri frowned. "What envelope?"

"Didn't I tell you? Otis left us some money, in case of emergencies."

I fumbled for the wad, but Ceri wasn't interested in the money. She was interested in the wifi.

"Can I go on Facebook?" she asked excitedly.

I stared at her in horror. What was it about being on the run she didn't get?

"Are you kidding? The site's got a GPS app. If those guys are media savvy, they can use it to locate us."

Ceri's face twitched. Maybe I was too stupid, maybe I was too infatuated with her, but I didn't pick up the signals.

I should have realised then that she'd done something stupid. I didn't get it. I just took it as another sign that she felt lost.

"Something wrong?"

"No, why would there be?"

"I don't know. For a moment you looked like you'd seen a ghost."

Ceri turned her back and gazed out of the window. Second time I didn't get it. Every time I think about what happened, I wonder how I could have been so slow on the uptake. Maybe if I'd been a bit more savvy, I could have stopped blood being spilled.

"It's just the mention of those men."

I watched her a while, wondering why she was acting so weird, then I shrugged and closed down the laptop.

"This thing is no use if they can track it."

Ceri was still at the window. She hesitated as if she had something to tell me.

"Are you sure there's nothing wrong?" I asked.

"I'm fine, OK?"

I flopped on to the sofa.

"Otis should be around soon."

But we wouldn't see Otis that morning.

Or the next day.

And that was down to Ceri.

I was in the toilet twenty minutes later when her voice

came clawing against the door. What now? Then the words took on form, meaning.

"John, you've got to get out of there."

"Come again?"

"Oh, wake up, will you? It's them!"

Them.

Weird how one word can scare the crap out of you.

Them.

A cold rush of fear ran down my spine. This couldn't be real. It had to be some kind of joke, but the tone of Ceri's voice said she was deadly serious. She was yelling.

"Oh my God, it's them. We've got to go!"

I yelled back, still unable to take it in. "I'm trying to pee here. You're giving me stage fright." I was struggling to process it. She had to be mistaken. "What the hell are you talking about?"

"The Lincoln, it's coming down the street. Oh my God, John, it's them. It's happening all over again." Her breath came out in tortured gasps. "They're parking up. You've got to get out of there now."

I stared at the toilet bowl.

"I can't come out like this!"

"I don't care if you come out with your willy in your hand. We've got to go."

Her voice left me in no doubt. I zipped my fly and stumbled out of the bathroom, still unable to believe they'd found us. I joined her at the window and swore. Loudly. There was no mistaking the vehicle.

"How? How is it even possible?"

It couldn't be. My insides boiled. Snakehead was already out of the car, tugging at a passer-by's sleeve, obviously checking the address. Fat Lad was struggling to hoist his buttocks off the passenger seat.

"Follow me. I've got an escape route."

I stuffed a few things in a carrier and we thundered down the stairs. I was first to the bottom, leading the way just as a foot crashed against the front door. Ceri howled with fright. I put my weight against the lock and felt another kick threatening to smash it right off.

"That way!"

This time it was Ceri who was hesitating, paralysed with fright.

"Move!"

Snakehead booted the door a third time then he barked a command. The door was shuddering against my shoulder. One more good, hard kick and he would be inside.

"They're in there!" Snakehead yelled. "I can hear them."

There was a grunt of pain as he mistimed his next assault on the door. I could hear him hopping backwards in pain.

"See if there's a back way."

There was the sound of flat-footed running. Fat Lad would take time to get round the back. It gave me confidence. I bundled Ceri into the backyard and yelled my defiance.

"Way ahead of you, scumbag. Come on, you ugly tosser. Catch us if you can."

Ceri's eyes widened, hazel pools in a face so white and pinched it was as if she was turning into a ghost before my eyes.

"What are you doing?" she croaked, her voice shrunk to a tiny flake of sound.

I spelt it out. "I'm letting Beavis and Butthead know we're not scared."

In contrast to Ceri's crushed, hoarse murmur of terror, I was loud. I was as scared as she was, of course. I just showed it differently. I unlatched the gate and led the way into the alley. Ceri turned towards Sefton Park Road.

"No," I told her. "That's what they'll be expecting. This way."

There was a wall with broken glass embedded in cement. I tossed my jacket over the jagged shards and scrambled to the top. Ceri stared.

"I can't get up *there*," she yelped "It's too high!"

I thrust a hand her way. "Do you want them to catch you?"

"But . . ."

"Yes or no?"

"No."

One good heave and I had her crouching beside me on top of the wall.

"Did you have all this planned?" she demanded, staring down at the alley.

"It was Otis's idea. You've got to have a back-up plan."

Suddenly I was enjoying the way Ceri looked at me. I dropped down the other side. She followed.

"Where are we going?"

"We're working our way round."

"Why? We could run into them."

"And we could outwit them. Got a better idea?"

"Yes, phone the police twelve hours ago."

I snorted. "Oh, nice thinking. I left my Tardis at home. Let's go."

We scampered through the gardens, darting anxious glances every which way. We emerged cautiously on to the main road just as a taxi came down the street.

"Joe!" I yelled. "Joe Baxi!"

The taxi indicated and pulled over.

"Where to?"

"Anywhere! Just drive."

The taxi driver's brow crumpled.

"Who do you think you are, son, James Bond? Now stop playing silly beggars." A cautious look. "You do have money?"

Ceri was craning to look down the street.

"Snakehead just came out of the alley," she hissed. "Show the man some money. Do it!"

I followed the direction of her stare. Snakehead was still looking the other way, oblivious to our presence. Any moment now, he was going to spot us. I peeled a twenty from the wad.

"This do?"

Snakehead was still turning, searching for some sign of us. My eyes were pleading for the driver to come to a decision.

"OK," he said. "Where to?"

This time, Ceri took the lead.

"Town."

"Where in town?"

"I'll tell you when we're closer. Quickest route. Now go. Please."

The taxi driver gave us the once-over, his gaze full of caution then he put the vehicle in first gear.

He started to pull away from the kerb.

"I don't know what game you're playing, but a fare's a fare."

At the end of the road, we checked the street. Snakehead was turning. I saw his eyes clock us and he was yelling for Fat Lad to shift himself. I leaned forward to talk to the driver.

"Can't you go any faster?"

He made with the dead eyes. "I don't know what's going on here, but I'm not breaking any speed limits on account of a couple of kids."

My heart was pounding. There was still no sign of the Lincoln. Suddenly, I realised where we were. I saw the bombed-out church up ahead.

"Stop!"

"Come again?"

"Stop the cab. We'll walk from here."

"What are you doing?" Ceri demanded.

"The speed we're doing, the Gruesome Brothers will have no problem catching us. Trust me. We've got to bail."

Ceri looked back. "OK."

I shoved the twenty in the driver's hand, grabbed Ceri's arm and led her down a side road.

The taxi driver was shouting. "What about your change?"

"Keep it. Just drive, OK? Keep going. That's what I'm giving you the extra for. So we can get away."

The driver stared for a moment then he drove off.

I bundled Ceri into a gateway. "Stay there. Keep out of sight."

"What are you going to do?"

"See if they're following us."

I was edging to the end of the street when the Lincoln roared past in pursuit of the taxi. I flattened myself against the wall and watched it go. I almost burst out laughing, but there was no time to savour the moment.

"We need to shift. We don't have long."

"We did it," Ceri whispered in triumph.

"Yes. Skin of our teeth. How in God's name did they know about the flat?"

Ceri flashed me a hostile stare. "What are you asking me for? The point is, they did. They always find us. So much for Otis."

She had just put into words my worst nightmare, that

everything I had ever known was a lie. If I couldn't trust Otis and Jimmy, I might as well lie down and die. They were my blood brothers. If they could betray me . . . No, it wasn't them. It couldn't be.

"What, you don't trust me now?"

Ceri plucked a lock of hair from the corner of her mouth.

"I'm starting to wonder if I can trust anybody. You dragged me down to Liverpool 8. You told me I'd be safe and those animals still found us. I'm way out of my comfort zone here."

"You and me both."

"Oh, is that right? Who's got a gangster for a father?"

"He isn't a gangster. He got caught up in something. He . . ."

Who was I trying to kid? Maybe gangster is exactly what he was.

"He's just a minor player, is that what you're saying?" Ceri's hazel eyes were blazing. "Just don't talk for a while. I don't trust you. Every time I decide to do something half sensible, you stop me."

I halted.

"OK, if that's the way you want it, go. Start walking. I won't try to stop you. Go."

Ceri seemed uncertain.

"You think it's all down to me?" I said. "Fine, do one. See if I care."

"Don't tell me what to do," she yelled. "I've had it with your advice. It's my turn to make the decisions."

Ceri was right about one thing. Until we knew what was going on, we couldn't trust anybody. We were on our own.

"John, are you listening?"

My mind was in turmoil. Snakehead and Fat Lad couldn't have found us, unless . . . I squeezed my eyes shut. The only possible explanation didn't bear thinking about.

"Are you accusing Otis?" I growled under my breath.

"I thought you were going to keep your trap shut. It's my turn to call the shots."

"But where . . .?"

"Oh, just shut up! Leave it to me, will you?"

I lapsed into a grudging silence and followed Ceri.

Lime Street is a busy station. There are statues of Bessie Braddock and Ken Dodd on the concourse. She was a politician. He's a comedian. That's the sum total of my Wiki knowledge. We stood next to them, flotsam and jetsam in a human tide. I wondered what Doddy was doing with a feather duster in his hand. Ceri wondered whether we would get to live out the day. We watched all the purposeful people with a kind of numb detachment. I had never felt more vulnerable in my life. It was as if Snakehead and Fat Lad were going to emerge from the crowd at any moment. The idea made my flesh crawl. My gaze was flying this way and that.

"Do you think they're still following us?"

"How should I know? I can't believe it's only been one day since life was normal."

Still, I scrutinised the crowd. Every time there was a bald guy, a fat guy – well, a guy – my heart missed a beat.

"How much cash have you got?" Ceri asked, breaking in on my thoughts.

"Not sure."

"You mean you haven't even counted it?"

I shook my head. The thought never even occurred to me. Otis would see us right. That's what he did. He'd dragged my dad's arse out of the fire more than once. He wasn't the one who told those men where we were. It couldn't be him. It just couldn't. It would be like the Pope turning atheist.

"You're unbelievable," Ceri snorted.

She had this way of making me feel like a complete moron.

"It's a roll of tens and twenties. Couple of hundred maybe, something like that."

"A couple of hundred! Otis gave you all that money?"

I heard the disbelief in her voice and I realised that we lived in completely different worlds.

"Like I said, Otis and Jimmy, they're family." A moment's hesitation. "As good as."

That's when I broke off. Why hadn't I realised earlier?

"Oh, I don't believe it! Crap, crap, crap. Oh, you idiot!"

"What now?"

I saw people looking.

"I've really done it this time. In all the panic to get out of the flat, I got my phone and the camera, but I left my laptop behind. I downloaded the photos. They'll see them."

"Not without a password."

I had a confession to make.

"I forget passwords. It's *Password123*."

"You have got to be kidding?"

"I wish."

"Why are boys such morons?"

Who was arguing?

Ceri shrugged.

"I don't see how this changes anything. They know what we've got."

"It changes one thing," I told her. "I can't use my phone. They'll have my Facebook and Instagram details. They can track it."

I had her attention.

"You said something like that in the flat. How does it work?"

There it was again and still I didn't get it.

"I don't know the details. There's an app on Facebook for definite. My dad was in a hotel in Yorkshire and a mate of his messaged him: 'How's Leeds?' It freaked him out until his friend explained that Facebook has GPS."

I turned the phone off and removed the battery.

"What are you doing?" Ceri demanded.

"Making dead sure."

"Will it work?"

I shrugged.

"You don't know much about tech, do you?"

"Ha, and you do?"

Ceri conceded defeat.

"OK, John. You've convinced me. We go missing. How long for?"

"Just a day," I told her. "Dad gets in tomorrow morning some time."

"So we go missing until then?"

"Right. We've only got to stay out of harm's way for twenty-four hours. How hard can that be?"

Ceri rolled her eyes. "Do you want me to answer that? We haven't done too well so far, have we?"

"Good point."

"Looks like we have to settle for Plan Otis. We've been doing this all wrong."

"How do you mean?"

"We've been staying on home turf."

"What are you saying?"

"We get out of Liverpool altogether." She inspected the departures board. "There's a train in a few minutes. Plan Otis it is. Radio silence, phone silence, John silence, whatever name you want to put on it."

This was new. There was no more talk of contacting the police. I had a feeling more was going on than staying safe. At first, she'd been scared witless. Suddenly, she seemed to be enjoying the chase. I didn't get it at all.

"From now on," Ceri said, with a flick of her hair, "I call the shots."

After the L8 disaster, I was all out of options. I knew in my bones that Otis and Jimmy would never sell me down the river, but what other explanation was there? How had they found us? For the time being, Ceri was the boss.

"You've got it. Where are we going?"

"I'm not telling you." She stuck out a hand. "You'll find out once we're on the train. Show me the money, honey."

What had come over quiet, nervous Ceri? I dug my hand in my pocket and stripped off a few notes. Ceri set off in the direction of the ticket office.

"So I wait here, yeah?"

She flapped her hand in the air, dismissing my words with contempt.

"Whatever."

I was still watching the crowd, imagining Snakehead and Fat Lad shoving their way towards us.

"You're not going to go missing again?"

"You don't own me. I'll do what I like."

I shouted after her. "You are getting me a ticket though?"

She turned. "You want one?"

Why did I feel like a dog who'd peed on the carpet? "Yes, I want one."

She was on her way back when I recognised a face in the crowd. I yelled a warning. "Ceri!"

It was too late. He had hold of her arm. I was running.

"Let go of her!"

Faces rushed around me. The sounds of the station boomed in my head.

"Let her go!"

It was the taxi driver. When I started pulling at his arm, he held his hands up.

"There's no need to flip. I'm not going to do her any harm."

I scanned the crowd. Where was Snakehead? The driver was still talking.

"Look, I saw your friend when I pulled into the rank. You can hardly miss that hair."

I didn't trust him. I didn't trust anybody any more. I was searching for any sign of Snakehead and Fat Lad.

"You promise you haven't led them to us?"

He seemed horrified.

"You've got to be kidding. Why would I? They put the fear of God into me."

Could we trust him? "They must have caught up with you, though."

"They did. They forced me to pull over. You see some things on the cabs, but these guys, they're something else. What the hell have you two got yourselves into? They're not the kind of people you want to walk into on a dark night."

Ceri gave a nervous laugh. "We worked that out already."

I was still feeling exposed. "You're sure you haven't led them to us?"

The taxi driver shook his head. "Listen, son, I had no

information to give them. They flashed me and made me stop the cab. They wanted to know where I dropped you. They gave me a right grilling."

"But you didn't say anything?"

"I didn't know anything." He looked over his shoulder. I guessed one of the other drivers was watching his cab. "I said I dropped you at Paddy's Wigwam. Thought it would give you some breathing space."

Ceri beamed. "Thank you so much!"

"It's pure chance I saw you at the ticket office. It just so happened I was pulling up at the rank. Listen, I've got a daughter about your age. Whatever trouble you're in, I'm not the kind of guy to shop a couple of kids."

Ceri nodded. "Thank you."

She believed him. I didn't say a word.

The taxi driver laughed. "I didn't do anything."

He started to walk away.

"Hey," Ceri called. "What's your name?"

"Danny. Danny O'Brien."

"See you, Danny O'Brien."

I was still wondering whether to trust him. "What in God's name was that about?"

"A nice guy," Ceri said simply. "Somebody who cares. Ready to go?"

I held my hand out. "I'll take my ticket."

Ceri shook her head. "You can have it when we board the train."

"What?"

"You heard. You wanted us to vanish off the face of the world? Your little trip on Merseyrail was pathetic."

"Why was it?"

"Think about it. You said yourself, your dad knew the guy on the beach. So what do you do? You take us back to his old stamping ground. What kind of idiot tries to turn invisible by going somewhere they're known?"

"I'm not an idiot," I growled.

Ceri ignored my protests.

"If you want to do it properly, I'll show you how. Are you up for this?"

Up for what? I wondered. She was right, though. Everything I'd touched had turned to crap.

"I suppose."

"Fine. I'm in charge. I call the shots. I keep the tickets."

The new Ceri was winding me up.

"Stop treating me like a kid!"

She snorted. "Stop acting like one."

I pulled her to one side. "You're blaming me for those two turning up at the flat."

Ceri paused. "You dragged us down there, John. You persuaded me the safe house was the best option. You persuaded me it was *safe*. We're there a few hours and they turn up. That means somebody spilled their guts." She poked me in the chest. "Somebody you know." She held out her hand. "I keep the phone."

"No way. It's mine," I snapped. "You only want it to phone that Gemma."

I got a reaction. Maybe it should have got me thinking, but I seemed to be missing all the signals. Ceri gnawed at her bottom lip as she considered the situation.

"OK, I keep the battery. You keep the phone. We're in this together."

"I don't get it."

"I saw it in an old film once. Two people have half a sixpence each."

"That's stupid."

"Why's it stupid? Hear me out, will you?"

"Why've they got half each?"

"I don't remember," she admitted, "but I suppose it means we share the responsibility. There are no phone calls unless we both agree to them."

Finally, I slapped the battery in Ceri's palm. "I'll go along with it . . . for now."

"It's about time," Ceri said. "I've gone along with your mad schemes and look where it's got us."

She shoved the battery in her jacket pocket and zipped it up. "Let's board the train."

I read the destination board. "Chester. What's in Chester?"

"The zoo."

"Seriously? We're going to look at animals?"

"Don't be stupid. We're not going to the zoo."

"You said!"

"I said Chester's got a zoo, divvy!"

I found myself wondering how we'd got here.

"What then?"

"I'll tell you when we get there."

"This is stupid."

Ceri turned. "You think?" She lowered her voice. "You're the one who wouldn't phone the police. You're the one whose dad got us into this hell. You're the one who put us in a safe house that wasn't. Still wonder why I want to take precautions?"

I tried to think of something to say, but I was all out of ideas. "Chester it is."

We found seats opposite each other. As the train pulled out of the station, I started humming tunelessly.

"What's that?" Ceri asked.

"Call yourself a Scouser? Don't you recognise it?"

Ceri kicked at my foot.

"Call yourself musical? No, I don't. *Match of the Day* theme?"

I rolled my eyes.

"*Match of the Day*! Behave, will you? It's the *Leaving of Liverpool*."

AWAY

We stood on the station platform, near-strangers thrown together by circumstances. We had a plan. At least Ceri did. Go to this hiding place of hers, wherever it was, stay out of sight for twenty-four hours, meet Dad, put family back together. The stakes were high. I couldn't get that image out of my mind: Snakehead's outstretched arm, the weapon, the victim. Then, in the shadows, I saw my own family, that swinging light bulb, the bare room and again, that outstretched arm. I forced the thought from my mind.

"Are you going to tell me where we're going?"

Ceri ignored me. She was busy buying a packet of chewing gum. She offered a piece and I turned it down. Something occurred to me.

"Hey, where's the change from the tickets?"

"Right here in my pocket," Ceri said. "I'm keeping it."

I was about to object, but Ceri cut me off.

"It isn't your money. Didn't you say it was for both of us, to keep us out of trouble? Well, I am half of the people in trouble."

I was losing control and I didn't like the feeling. "Otis put me in charge."

"Hello," Ceri shot back. "This is the twenty-first century, Mr El Sexismo. I've got some say in this."

"Who are you calling sexist?"

"Now, let me see, YOU!!"

"Whoa, unexpected gobby girl in the bagging area!"

"Who are you calling gobby?"

I stood my ground.

"Oh, I'm thinking the redhead who's got trouble written right through her like a stick of rock and a mouth yay wide."

I held out my arms to illustrate the point. Ceri wasn't backing off.

"Says the stubborn moron who got us into this mess in the first place. Who wouldn't phone the police? Who dragged us off to some stupid flat instead of calling 999? Who said we were safe but, guess what, Happy and Clappy turned up a few hours later." She watched my face. "No answer, huh? I didn't think so. Stand down, soldier."

I was about to argue back when it dawned on me that I still didn't have an answer to my original question. I gave up on the money and changed the subject.

"Where are we going? What's in Chester?"

Ceri turned on her heel and examined the platform indicator.

"Nothing's in Chester." Then she said, as an afterthought, "Well, there are lots of things in Chester, but there's nothing

104

to keep us here. This is where we get our connection. We're going to Wales."

"Wales? What the hell are we going there for?"

Ceri checked nobody was listening, planted her hands on her hips and spelt it out.

"One, it isn't Liverpool. Two, it's miles away from Liverpool. Three, those murdering scum aren't going to find us there. Four . . . Well, I'll tell you about Four on the train."

She told me about Four as the train picked up speed on its westward journey.

"We're going to my favourite place in the whole world."

I waited for her explanation.

"There's this lovely, little B&B . . ."

"That's it? Your big idea is a bed and breakfast?"

Ceri brought me back to reality.

"Your big idea worked out well. They found us."

She had a point. She took my silence as acceptance of her plan.

"So we go the whole hog and get the hell out of Liverpool. Mrs Jones will see us right."

"Mrs Jones?"

"The woman who runs the B&B. Were you not listening?" She cocked her head. "Do you want to be safe or what?"

More than anything. I wanted to be safe myself and I wanted to know what had happened to my family. Right then, if I'm perfectly honest, I wanted somebody else's life. More than once I'd been tempted to ask Ceri for my phone battery, but there was that message from Otis. If everything went pear-shaped, find somewhere to hide while things got sorted. It seemed the right thing to do, but it failed to dislodge the gnawing ball of anxiety in my gut. Somebody had given those men our location and there weren't many candidates.

"So this Mrs Jones, she'll put us up?"

"Of course she'll put us up. She runs a B&B."

Oh, this was getting better all the time. This Mrs Jones, she wasn't even helping us out of the goodness of her heart.

"You mean we've got to pay for rooms?"

Ceri's voice told me she hadn't even thought about money. "I suppose so."

"What's that going to cost?"

She definitely hadn't thought it through. "I don't know."

I had my mouth wide open.

"Oh, this is a good plan. Rooms are, what, fifty quid, sixty?"

"We've got enough to cover it."

"It won't take long to clear us out of cash the way you're spending it. What happens then? What about food? What about getting back to Liverpool?"

Ceri had an answer to that one, at least. "We're only going to be there one night. Plus I bought return tickets."

"OK, what about *food*?"

"There's an all-you-can-eat breakfast at the B&B. Fill your boots."

I thought of something.

"Have you been in touch with this Mrs Jones?"

"Not for a while."

By then my BS detector was maxing out.

"When's the last time you talked to her?"

Ceri's gaze drifted out of the window, watching the landscape rush by.

"Ceri?"

"She'll put us up. She's really nice."

A thick knot of frustration filled my throat.

"When, Ceri? When did you last talk to her?"

A young mum across the aisle was rocking her baby, trying to stop him crying. Ceri focused on the scene for a moment. There was no answer.

"Don't ignore me, Ceri. I want to know when. Summer?"

Still no answer.

"Easter?"

By now the silence was deafening. She had to be kidding.

"*Christmas*?"

Ceri didn't answer directly.

"I was happy there. You don't understand. I was happy at my nan's house. I was happy at Mrs Jones's B&B. They're the only places I've ever been happy."

I wasn't feeling too good about the direction of this conversation.

"What, you went there on holiday? You were her regulars, is that what you're saying? Talk to me, Ceri. I'm in the middle of nowhere and I want to know the reason."

Ceri folded her arms and met my look. "I was ten, if you really want to know."

"Ten!"

I was dumbstruck. Finally, I recovered enough to say something.

"That's six years ago."

"Hey, Mr Genius passed his maths test."

We'd both started to raise our voices. Knowing somebody might be listening, I moved seats and whispered in her ear.

"You went there *once*?"

She folded her arms stubbornly.

"That's what I said."

My voice was rising again. Something didn't stack up. OK, so I wasn't exactly being straight with Ceri, but she was definitely hiding things from me too.

"Am I hearing you right? We're going on the off-chance that this woman remembers a girl who visited for a week, six years ago? That's nuts. She might not even run the place any more. Have you thought of that?"

Ceri kept her arms folded across her chest, gaze fixed on the seat opposite. "She'll be there."

I held my head. I couldn't believe what I was hearing.

"Now we're in the world of wishful thinking."

"Anyway," Ceri said. "It wasn't a week. It was a weekend."

Just when I thought it couldn't get any more absurd, it just had. "Two days! Am I hearing you right? You were there *two* days?"

Ceri leaned her forehead on the windowpane.

"You don't understand. I was happy. Mum took me. We felt like a family."

She only went for a weekend and suddenly it's this magic refuge? What was wrong with her?

I snorted. "So you keep saying."

She struggled on regardless. "Somehow, being away from Liverpool made Mum a different person. There were no men around. She was nice to me."

I wanted to grab Ceri by the shoulders and shake her out of the dream world she'd crawled into.

"And she wasn't usually nice to you?"

Ceri shook her head, brow still pressed against the glass.

"Are you crying?"

She rubbed at her eyes. "No."

"Yes, you are."

"So why ask?"

I handed her a tissue. "Look, please don't get upset. I don't like seeing you upset."

She inspected the tissue with some suspicion.

"It's clean. I didn't blow my nose on it."

"Yewww."

"I said I *didn't*!"

Ceri wiped her tears away and blew her nose. "I know what you said."

She offered to return the tissue. I laughed.

"You're kidding, right? I don't want it after you've snotted all over it."

It was her turn to laugh. She shoved the tissue in her pocket. That's when I asked my question. "Did she hit you – your mum, I mean?"

Ceri replied with only a slight hesitation. "Not so much."

"So she did?"

There was a grudging admission.

"Sometimes. She hated her life. I was the only one around so she took it out on me. Do we have to talk about this?"

Somehow, we did. "It was drugs, wasn't it?"

Ceri nodded absently, drifting into a past she didn't want to revisit.

"She was OK until she got hooked." She fished for the tissue. "Look, can we discuss this another time?"

I returned to the seat opposite and leaned against the headrest, closing my eyes.

"Sure. Whatever you say."

Ceri leaned forward. "Are you angry with me?"

"Not particularly." Liar. I wanted to kick the holy crap

out of something. "I think you're crazy, but nice crazy. You do stupid things, but stupid things are happening." I sat forward again. "Here's how it is. I'm fed up of being on the run. I'm frightened for my family. I don't even know what we're doing here. The whole thing is completely unreal."

I felt her hand on my knee and squinted at her. Ceri realised she was touching my leg. She also knew the message it was giving out. She sat back in her seat, placing both palms on her thighs.

"Don't get the wrong idea. I just wanted to get your attention, nothing else."

I smiled. She had my attention . . . and some.

"You did that, all right." I let a few seconds go by. "Listen, I don't know how those guys found us, but it wasn't Otis. I've known him all my life."

Ceri wasn't impressed. "People change."

"Not Otis." If he could rat us out, then the whole world was rotten. It didn't bear thinking about. "I've known him all my life. He's as true as steel."

"But those men found us. Forget the emotion, John. Put loyalty aside. Can you explain that?"

I had no answer. "No, I can't."

After that, we were each lost in our own thoughts. We didn't speak. We didn't make eye contact. In fact, we didn't exchange a single word until the train pulled into the next station.

Llandudno.

*

111

Mrs Jones's B&B wasn't hard to find. Ceri knew the address. *Some memory*, I thought. The third person we asked was local and he was able to direct us. As we turned into the street, Ceri's eyes lit up.

"This is it. It's exactly how I remember it."

I listened to the joy in her voice and struggled to match her reaction with the scene before me. It was a very ordinary row of houses and bungalows. Two of them were B&Bs. The second one belonged to Mrs B. Jones. Ceri stopped at the gate and stared at the bungalow.

"Well, what's stopping you?" I asked. "Why don't you knock?"

Ceri hesitated. There was the sound of a dog barking inside.

"Ceri," I reminded her, "you dragged us all the way from Liverpool to come here. What's the problem? Is it the dog?"

"No, I like dogs."

"So what's the hold-up?"

Ceri shut me out. The expression in her eyes was intense and unreadable. In the event, the next move was decided for us. A curtain twitched and the front door opened. A woman in her mid-fifties stood on the doorstep, wiping her hands with a paper towel. A Labrador tumbled out and started to snuffle at Ceri's legs. Its tail thumped back and forth. Ceri instinctively reached down and patted the animal.

"Can I help you?" the woman asked. "I saw you from the window."

Ceri was still rubbing at the dog's neck. She flicked a nervous glance my way then she spoke.

"It's me, Ceri."

I couldn't believe my ears. Not: "do you have vacancies?" Not: "do you have any rooms?" Mrs Jones looked puzzled. No wonder. She puts a snotty-nosed kid up for the weekend. Six years later, the snotty-nosed kid is a troubled teenager and she turns up expecting to be remembered.

"Ceri? Should I . . .?"

By now, Ceri was kneeling, wrapping her arms round the dog's neck, pressing her cheek against its fur.

"I stayed here once. I wasn't very old. You said I was your little flame." Ceri let the dog go and plucked at her hair. "On account of this."

Mrs Jones searched her memory, then there was the ghost of a smile moving across her face.

"Ceri. Yes. I do remember. You were with your mother . . ."

The smile faltered. I stepped into the gaping silence.

"What Ceri's trying to say is, do you have any vacancies?" I produced the wad of cash. "We've got money."

Mrs Jones stared at the notes and told me to put my money away.

"Is there anybody with you?"

Ceri shook her head. "No. It's just us."

"I'm sorry, but I can't offer you rooms. How old are you? Fifteen?"

"Sixteen," I said. "Ceri, we should go."

Ceri didn't move. The dog had wandered back over and she was scratching its head absently.

"Please, Mrs Jones," she said tearfully. "I was happy here. I thought you would . . ."

Finally, the tears came, not rare ones like darts of rain in the wind, but floods accompanied by choking sobs. "You . . ."

Then she couldn't say any more. Mrs Jones watched her for a moment then stepped aside to let us enter the bungalow.

"Come inside. We can't talk on the doorstep."

She led us into a neat, comfortable lounge. There was a widescreen TV on the wall and magazines fanned out on a coffee table. Mrs Jones waved at the sofa. I took my seat, followed by Ceri. The Labrador flopped down at Ceri's feet.

"Another tissue?" I offered.

Ceri laughed through her tears. Mrs Jones watched her for a moment then sat down in the armchair opposite, resting her hands on the taut platform of her skirt.

"Are you two in trouble?"

"No!" That was too loud. I toned it down. "No."

"You don't have any adults with you," Mrs Jones observed. "You don't have any luggage."

"My nan is dying," Ceri said. "My mum is, well, you remember my mum, don't you?"

Mrs Jones gave a brief nod. Clearly, she did. What

114

was so memorable about Ceri's mother, that this woman remembered her when she only stayed for two days, six years ago? Mrs Jones tried another question.

"Are you two . . .?" She struggled for the right word. "Are you together?"

Ceri laughed as she dabbed at her tears. "No way!"

That didn't do my self-esteem any good. Did she really have to be in such a hurry to dismiss the idea?

"What is it you want, Ceri?"

Ceri stared fixedly at the carpet then met Mrs Jones's gaze.

"I want sanctuary."

"Sanctuary?"

"I want somebody to trust me enough to let me stay, just for one day. No questions asked." Then she added a pointed finale. "Just for tonight."

Mrs Jones considered Ceri's appeal. She seemed reluctant, but it was obvious that ten-year-old Ceri James had made an impression, or maybe it was her mother who had left her mark. Mrs Jones put her hand to her mouth as she thought. After some time, she breathed through her fingers and made a decision.

"You can stay," she said, "just for one night, but it has got to be in separate rooms."

"Of course," Ceri said, clearly horrified that any other arrangement was possible. "It was never going to be any other way. It isn't like that."

For the second time, I pulled out the wad of cash.

"Put that away," Mrs Jones told me. "Guests pay on departure. Have you eaten?"

"Chocolate cakes," Ceri said.

"Brioches," I said, correcting her.

"For breakfast."

"Breakfast? You haven't eaten since then?"

"No."

"Stay here," Mrs Jones said. "I'll make you some sandwiches. Is turkey salad OK?"

Ceri smiled. "That sounds lovely."

Mrs Jones stopped at the door.

"Oh, and you can call me Bethan while you're here." She glanced at the dog. "You're a hit with Tilly Mint."

"Tilly Mint," Ceri said. "Is that her name?"

"Yes, we didn't have her the last time you visited. She's Tilly for short."

Ceri watched Mrs Jones go then turned to me.

"Didn't I tell you? She's lovely, isn't she?"

"You must have nine lives, Ceri James. I can't believe you've talked your way into staying."

Ceri managed a smile. "I think I cried my way into it."

"You got that right. Nice trick. I wish I could do it."

"It wasn't a trick," Ceri protested.

We sat in silence until our sandwiches arrived. There were two rounds each, with crisps at the side and glasses of orange juice. There were even flapjacks.

"I made them myself," Mrs Jones informed us.

"Real little Mary Berry," I observed.

The flapjacks were oozing honey. I wanted to skip the sandwiches and get down to the sweet stuff.

"See, I knew you were a big softy." Ceri leaned forward to whisper something to Mrs Jones. "He's got a soggy bottom."

I took the ribbing. It was good to see Ceri happy. Sitting there, fed and comfortable, Tilly lying at Ceri's feet, it was possible to push the thoughts of Liverpool, the shooting and my family to the back of my mind, if only for a few moments. The sun streamed through the windows and I knew why Ceri found this place so reassuring. Every item of furniture, every photo on the walls, every neatly arranged vase of flowers breathed something neither Ceri or I had ever really known.

Security.

"Is there a Mr Jones, Bethan?"

Mrs Jones shook her head.

"No, my husband died of a heart attack eight years ago. He was only young. I'm on my own now." She gestured to a row of photographs in a unit against the wall. There were graduation pictures. "My son lives in South Africa. My daughter works in London." She looked around. "I've got Tilly for company and the B&B keeps me busy. The business is my life now. I get some lovely guests."

"Mum wasn't one of them, was she?" Ceri asked.

Mrs Jones didn't know how to answer.

"Your mum had had a difficult life. I don't judge people, Ceri. You love her and . . ."

Ceri interrupted. "I don't. I don't love her. I hate her. I haven't seen her in . . . I haven't seen her since forever. My gran is the only person who has ever cared about me. And Gemma."

Mrs Jones didn't ask who Gemma was. She didn't say anything in response to Ceri's sudden outburst. She did glance my way, clearly wondering how I fitted into the picture. Ceri endured several moments' uncomfortable silence then, in a quiet voice, she apologised.

"I'm sorry."

Mrs Jones patted Ceri's small hands.

"There's nothing to be sorry about." She stood. "I'll show you to your rooms. You can freshen up. It's a lovely day outside. You might want to walk along the seafront."

Ceri nodded. "I'd like that."

Mrs Jones showed Ceri to her room and explained about the bedroom and front-door keys, breakfast times and where the best places to go were. Once Ceri was safely installed in her room, Mrs Jones led me across the landing.

"This is great," I said, gazing at the double bed and comfortable furnishings. "It's got an en-suite bathroom and everything." I looked out of the window. "Nice view too."

Mrs Jones heard me out. She paid little interest to the positive comments. She was more interested in what had brought us here.

"John, you don't have to tell me why you're here, but it is only right if there is something I should know. I could get myself into hot water."

I couldn't think how anything about our situation could get Mrs Jones – Bethan – into trouble, so that's what I told her.

"There's no problem," I said. "It's complicated. It was right what you said before. Ceri's got issues."

"That's what you are then," Mrs Jones said. "Someone to watch over her."

"Yes, I'm her guardian angel."

Mrs Jones walked to the door then turned. "Take care of that young lady. She's been hurt."

I nodded. "Yes, I know."

Mrs Jones hesitated. "Is Sean still around?"

My face betrayed me. Mrs Jones saw the frown.

"So you don't know Sean?"

"No, Ceri never mentioned any Sean. Is there something I should know?"

Mrs Jones glanced away.

"Forget I ever said anything. Really, I shouldn't have mentioned it."

She was gone before I could say another word. The mention of this guy Sean had an impact and not a good one. Ceri knocked a few minutes later and stood uncertainly in the doorway. I saw the delay.

"I won't jump on you, you know," I said.

"I know you won't. Sorry I've been so hard on you."

This was new. Charm offensive? Still, it was promising. I tried to keep my answer non-committal. "Have you?"

"I think so. Anyway, I'm not sure if Bethan will like it, us being in the room with the door shut."

I kicked a wooden door wedge in place to keep it open. "How's that?"

Ceri pulled a face. "It doesn't sound right, calling her Bethan. She was always Mrs Jones."

"She's OK, your Mrs Jones."

Ceri beamed. We didn't seem to have agreed much since the scene on the beach. It was good to be on the same wavelength.

"We should do something," she said.

I wanted to ask about this Sean, but it seemed wrong to ruin the moment.

"Such as?"

"Well, we're at the seaside. We could walk on the beach, take off our shoes and paddle. I'm going to kick sand in your face."

I grinned. "Yes, you and whose army?"

We looked in on Mrs Jones. She was humming along to a tune on the radio.

"Hi, Bethan," Ceri said, still self-conscious about using Mrs Jones's first name. "We're going out. We won't be long."

"Enjoy yourselves," Mrs Jones said. "The Great Orme is the obvious destination."

Ceri took a punt. "Can we take Tilly out for a walk?"

Mrs Jones smiled. "Why not? Her lead is on the hook over there. Her ball's on the table in a pot. She likes chasing it."

I gave the radio a rueful glance. "What's that you're listening to?"

Mrs Jones laughed. "It just came on. *Tie a Yellow Ribbon*. Something to do with soldiers coming home from the war."

"Which war?"

"I don't remember the details. People tied a yellow ribbon outside the house to welcome the men home."

"That's an idea," Ceri said. "If you see anything strange, you could tie a ribbon for us."

I wanted to throttle Ceri. Why did she have to open her mouth?

The smile drained from Mrs Jones's face. "So you are in trouble?"

"Ignore Ceri," I said hurriedly. "She's being silly."

I ushered Ceri out of the door and looked over my shoulder at Mrs Jones. The look she gave me was full of meaning.

"What was that?" I demanded once we were out of earshot. "We only just got those rooms and you go freaking her out."

Ceri accepted the criticism. "Sorry."

The beach was a ten-minute walk. We wandered along the shoreline, neither of us saying very much, neither of us needing to. From time to time, Ceri would throw Tilly her ball and the dog would go scampering after it. We were past the time when we needed to talk for the sake of it.

It was Ceri who broke the silence.

"Remember the last time we were on a beach?" she said.

That got a laugh.

"It was only yesterday."

Ceri slipped off her shoes and shoved her socks inside them. "It seems like a lifetime ago." She dipped her toes in the tide. "John, you might find this hard to understand, but I don't want to go back. Not now. Not ever."

I watched her paddling, her thin legs coated with damp sand, her feet picking through the lapping waves like a wading bird.

"Is it really that bad, living at Greenways?"

"This isn't about Greenways. Nobody's mean, or anything."

"What then?"

"Home is where somebody loves you," she said. "Nobody loves me."

I had my troubles, but one thing I had never doubted. My parents loved me with a fierce, strong fire. What was it like growing up like Ceri, knowing that your mother had tossed you aside like an old coat? I tried to imagine the hole where trust, loyalty and security are meant to be and the thought of it stung my eyes. Mrs Jones had talked about Ceri being hurt. That made her sound weak, vulnerable. No, that wasn't it at all. This girl was strong, strong in a way that humbled me. If I'd gone through half the stuff she had, I would be lying on the bed, crying my eyes out.

Suddenly she skipped along the waterline. "Ruby, Ruby, Rub-eee."

"What are you doing?"

"I'm singing. It was playing the last time we were here. It's an oldie. Kaiser Chiefs."

"Yes, I remember it."

I stared out across the waves.

"Penny for them," Ceri said.

I let my gaze travel along the promenade. "My thoughts? They're not even worth that much. We saw a man killed, Ceri."

"In another place, another time, another world."

"No, Ceri, in this one. We can't just forget who we are."

"You're thinking about your family, aren't you?" Ceri asked.

"Of course, I can't stop thinking about them. I get these pictures flashing up in my mind . . . and I'm at the seaside acting as if I don't have a care in the world."

"My gran will have had her operation by now," Ceri said. "She'll be wondering where I am."

"See," I said. "There is somebody who loves you."

"She's dying."

She produced the phone battery from her pocket.

"What do you think? You get in touch with your mum. I can call the hospital."

I didn't reject it out of hand. I was desperate to know what was happening back home.

"We can't. Not yet."

Ceri turned and gazed out to sea, suddenly quiet and distant.

"Are you OK?" I asked.

"What, other than being on the run, being abandoned by my cow of a mother and wondering if my nan is going to die? Yes, I couldn't be happier."

"Right, that does it. You need cheering up. Let's go and have some fun."

Fun was taking turns tearing round on dodgem cars and roaring with laughter. One of us would stay with Tilly Mint while the other went for a ride. While the rubber-skirted vehicles slammed into other drivers, all thoughts of the menacing blue Lincoln were banished, at least for a while.

Ceri steered well. I told her so.

"I should do," she said. "It's down to my granddad. He took me down to this abandoned airfield and taught me to drive a couple of years ago. Then he died. That's what happens. People leave me or they die."

"Right," I said. I'd had it with death and abandonment. "There's nothing I can do about the Grim Reaper, but I love cars." I leaned in and whispered. "We should steal one, be like those two women, Thelma and Louise."

Ceri grinned.

"So which are you, Thelma or Louise?"

"Ha ha." I led the way off the dodgem track. "Trouble is, car security is so good now you can't take them."

"Would you really nick a car?" Ceri asked.

"No, not really. I wouldn't know how. My dad's the only one in our family who ever walked on the wild side."

I turned and looked at the Great Orme.

"You know," I said. "I do like a big hill. Do you want to take a look up there?"

Ceri dug me in the ribs. "We can be the Llandudno Hillbillies."

Tilly wagged her tail. Ceri was smiling. We seemed to be getting on better.

The Great Orme was flat and green with some rocks, patches of brown scrub and yellow gorse. The sea stretched out before us, flat and tranquil and greyish blue. Where the sun shone, the water gleamed, like a shining sword laid flat on the surface. Ceri broke the silence.

"You know what you said earlier?"

"What was that? I say a lot of stuff."

"You felt guilty being here."

I tugged at the zip on my jacket, as if shutting out a sudden chill. "That's right. I do."

"I don't."

She fought with her hair, made wild by the blustery conditions, and tied it back.

"I don't feel one bit guilty. I could stay here for ever."

Ceri walked with her arms thrown out wide to catch the wind.

"This is a turn-up. Not long ago you were yelling at

me for not calling the police. You wanted to get back to Greenways, see your gran, you know, be done with all this."

"I'm not going back," Ceri said. "Not now. Not ever. I want things to be just as they are now. I wish this moment was all there was."

The wind boomed and tore at our clothes before dropping down again.

"People say you can't walk away from your troubles. You've got to work through them. Well, what if running away is exactly what I want to do?" She glanced my way. "You were right not to call the police. All that stuff back home, it doesn't feel real any more."

She waved her arm at the scene before us.

"This is real. We're free. Ruby, Ruby, Rubeeeee!"

I laughed. "Ceri, Ceri, Cereeeee!"

She gave me a shove and ran off. I caught up with her and swung her round. She felt good in my arms. I had a question. "What about your nan?"

"I love her more than anybody in the whole world," Ceri said, "but there's nothing I can do for her now. She's going to die, and then I'll be alone. Maybe that makes me free. I don't want to go back to the home."

I wanted to tell her she wasn't alone. From past experience, I knew it would go down like a lead balloon. She shrugged me away. "Don't tell me she's going to pull through. Don't even think about it. Life's never that good."

She walked through the treeless landscape, stubbornly ignoring me.

"We should keep running . . . for ever."

I followed, struck by the change in Ceri. "What would we live on?"

"We'd find something. We can work."

This was new. Ceri was talking about us, some kind of life together, even if it was a life on the run. Crazy dream that it was, it made my heart slam.

"Where would we live? Not at Mrs Jones's place. It's sixty quid a night . . . each."

Ceri gave a shake of the head, like somebody reacting to a wasp. "We'd find something."

"You need references, money. Ceri, you're not thinking straight."

Yes, as if thinking straight was what she wanted right then. She set off across the grass with Tilly bounding at her heels. I caught up with her. When did we swap places?

"What's come over you, Ceri? This is a dream. We had to get out of Liverpool, but it's home. It's calling us back. We're going. Tomorrow."

Ceri met me with the same fierce, stubborn passion. "I don't want to go back. Ever. I know that now. There's nothing to go back to."

She pointed, vaguely, as if trying to pick out Liverpool in the distance.

"You go back if you want to. I'm staying here."

I don't think she meant any of it. She knew as well as I did that the past had a way of catching up and pulling you back into its clutches. I didn't need to go on. She dropped her eyes.

"Just let me have today."

There was an echo of defeat in her voice.

"That's fine," I answered. "Tomorrow . . ." I patted my jacket where I had my phone. "Tomorrow we find out what's happening."

At that moment I became aware of the camera hanging round my neck.

"Hey, stand over there. I'll take your photo. Then you can take mine."

Ceri didn't move.

"I told you on the beach, I don't like having my photo taken."

"Why not? The lads at school think you're one of the fit girls."

"Is that how you talk about me? You choose who's fit and who isn't?"

I shrugged. "And you don't? Girls compare the lads."

She was scowling.

"It's not the same."

I knew better than to argue.

"Well, I don't like people talking about me."

"It's only a bit of fun."

"You think?"

I heard the change in her voice. This wasn't about whether I found her attractive. That much was obvious.

"Do you know how some guys look at girls? It's sick."

128

I didn't get it. This whole thing had come right out of the blue.

"What's all this about, Ceri?"

She threw up her arms and started running.

"Get away from me!"

"Ceri!" I shouted into the wind. "Ceri, hold up. What's wrong?"

I chased after her. I managed to get hold of her arm. She reacted as if she'd been electrocuted. She was lashing out with her fists.

"Get off me! Get off me!"

In the end, I had to step back, hands in the air as if it was a hold-up.

"I won't touch you, OK? Just calm down. I don't know what happened back there. If I did something wrong, I'm sorry." I let it sink in. "Just calm down, yeah?"

It took her a few moments before her voice was back to normal.

She turned my way. "Do you?"

"Do I what?"

"Do you think I'm . . . fit?"

I didn't know what to say. Was she about to kick off again?

"Do you fancy me?"

Now I was the one feeling uncomfortable.

"Come on, don't be coy."

"Yes, I like you. I did right from the start."

"Why?"

"Sorry?"

"Why do you fancy me?"

"I don't know." I was a ball of confusion. "It's not something you can pin down easily, is it?" My neck was burning. "Can we drop this?"

When you're in a hole you stop digging.

"Did I make you squirm?" she asked.

"A bit."

"Good. That's how I feel when I hear guys talking about me."

"Sorry."

She was hard to read. Finally, she relented over the camera. "OK, you can take my picture."

She struck a pose, blowing at a stray lock of hair. The storm had passed.

"Left a bit. Left again."

"Are you trying to make me walk off the edge?" Ceri demanded, giggling.

I joined in. "Yes, that's exactly what you do when you're taking somebody's picture."

A voice broke in on our conversation. "Would you like me to take the pair of you together?"

There was a middle-aged couple just a few metres away. When did they appear? The man held out his hand. I passed him the camera. Ceri looked aghast.

"Sure. Thanks."

As we huddled together, Ceri poked me.

"The photos," she hissed. "I thought we weren't going to let the camera out of our sight."

I waved her concerns away. "We haven't. It's right there. He's not going to look at them, is he? Stop being paranoid."

The newcomer heard us whispering and waited.

"Ready?" he asked.

He took a few photos then returned the camera. I've still got those shots on my laptop. I look at them most days. "It's beautiful up here, isn't it?"

"Yes, it's sound."

"I recognise that accent. You're from Liverpool, aren't you?"

I didn't like the questions. "Yes. Why?"

"Oh, nothing, I recognised the accent, that's all. I used to work in Maghull. Do you know it?"

Maghull is in the north end, on the way to Woollyback Land.

"I know of it."

The man hadn't finished. "First time in Llandudno?"

I said yes. Ceri said no. The guy laughed.

"Do you know why they call this headland the Great Orme?"

No, I thought, *but you're going to tell me*. He reminded me of one of the teachers at school, guy who'd swallowed Wiki.

"I've no idea."

I was willing the couple to go on their way and leave us alone.

"It's from the Norse, *ormr* meaning snake and *hofuth* meaning head." So far so geeky, but his punchline was like a kick in the gut. "It means Snakehead."

Did he just say Snakehead? I exchanged glances with Ceri. Her eyes were wide. The guy saw the reaction.

"Is something wrong?" he asked.

"No," I answered. "Nothing wrong. Look, we have to go."

I dragged Ceri away. She had big wide eyes on the couple. Once we were out of earshot, I let out a breath. "That was just weird. Where did that come from? Snakehead."

Ceri looked over her shoulder. "You don't think they're part of it, do you? What if it's some kind of threat?"

I observed the couple in their matching Barbour coats. "They don't look the part."

"So you're an expert on gangsters now?" She dropped her voice, realising that I just might be. "John, I don't like it."

We hurried across the spongy ground. There was a woman walking her dog. I hailed her.

"Now what are you doing?" Ceri whispered.

"Checking something."

Tilly approached.

"What's her name?" the woman asked. "This is Muppet."

"Tilly Mint."

I took advantage of the moment. "Do you live round here?"

"I do."

"We were arguing about how the Great Orme got its name. Do you know what it means?"

"I think it's got something to do with a worm or sea serpent."

"And the word Orme, is it Welsh?"

"Viking, I think." She smiled. "Is this some sort of school project?"

"No, nothing like that," I linked Ceri's arm. "We were curious, that's all."

Two minutes up the slope, I turned to her.

"See, what that guy said is right. There's nothing to worry about, Ceri. It was pure coincidence."

She shivered. "I don't like coincidences."

Coincidences.

Like a guy who shoves a note in your pocket and your dad's name is there.

I didn't like coincidences either. The mention of Snakehead was a shadow over the day. Like an omen.

We should have listened.

You know when a girl you fancy calls you a friend?

That.

Ceri sprang it on me in the middle of what should have been a romantic afternoon. That's how I had it planned, anyway. We struggled along the promenade through a strengthening wind, Tilly tugging at the lead.

"They've got palm trees! I wasn't expecting that."

It was good seeing Ceri sparkling-eyed and smiling.

It was like she was a completely different person. How come somebody who could be so vibrant spent so much time living under a cloud? We paused to watch the leaves threshing and rippling in the breeze.

"I remember the first time my mum saw them," Ceri murmured. "She said we were going to see some camels. I knew she was teasing."

I did my Egyptian sand dance. She jabbed me in the ribs with her elbow then knelt down and hugged Tilly.

"I wish I had a dog like her."

I wished she would hug me the way she hugged Tilly.

"You love dogs, don't you?"

That got the weirdest reaction. I was expecting Ceri to gush about her favourite pooches. Instead, a light went out in her eyes. It was like a door had slammed and my tongue was trapped in it.

"Sorry, did I say something wrong?"

"Just a bad memory, that's all."

I squeezed her shoulder. "I'm a good listener."

"You don't want to hear my problems."

"Try me."

Ceri let my words hang for a while then she made her way to the nearest bench. She sat down, huddled in her jacket. I joined her.

"You reminded me of my mum, something she did."

"Something bad?"

"With Mum it was always bad." Ceri scratched the back of Tilly's ears. "I grew out of a bad seed. There weren't many happy times when I was little. She bought me a puppy when I was eight."

Was I missing something? What was so bad about a puppy?

"Isn't that a happy memory?" I asked.

"The best. I loved that little dog. Her name was Tyke. She was a pug with a beautiful, squashed-in face. Soon after, Mum started using. Everything went to crap after that. She sold my dog so she could pay for a fix."

Somehow, I didn't want to hear the rest, but I'd told Ceri to share so I would have to hear her out.

"I ran down one morning and Tyke was gone. So was her basket, her lead, her ball, everything that could have reminded me of her. Mum had taken a pet I loved and sold her. She didn't leave me anything. I was supposed to forget I'd ever had Tyke in my life. How do you do that to a kid?" She went quiet for a moment before continuing. "When I started crying, Mum locked me in my room as a punishment. I didn't go to school that day, or the next. She left me to sob my eyes dry."

And I thought I had problems.

"That sucks. I'm so sorry."

A hardness came into Ceri's face. Her voice was impatient.

"What are *you* sorry about?"

"I don't know. I just wish you'd had a happier life, that's all."

Suddenly there was the opposite reaction. Somehow,

I'd turned it round and said the right thing. Ceri surprised me by throwing her arms round my neck. I could feel her cheek against mine. I let my fingers trail down her spine. She didn't seem to notice or care. It was hard to know how to react. I had never known anyone blow hot and cold the way she did.

"You're a good guy, John. I need a friend right now."

I loved the feel of her against me. I felt guilty about the sensations that were surging through me. I wanted my hands on her waist, her shoulders, kneading their way down her spine to the bottom of her back. Friend? That wasn't good. I was aching for her. After a while, she pulled back, leaving me confused and frustrated as hell.

"We're always talking about me," she said. "What are your parents like?"

That was a slap in the face.

"You mean other than kidnapped?"

"Let's not go there, John. Can't we just live in a bubble, pretend there's no world beyond this, no Liverpool, no dead man on the beach, no bad guys? I want to live in a dream. We're going to make our calls tomorrow. Until then, let's pretend this is all there is."

Pretend there is no Liverpool. Above us only sky. Her words reminded me how nuts everything was.

"If that's what you want."

"It is. So your parents, what are they like?"

I had to think about it.

"Mum's kind of, well, normal."

Ceri rolled her eyes. "Normal? What the hell is normal?"

Good question. There was nothing normal about my life, or hers. I still had the story of the dog going through my mind. It had made me feel really flat and depressed. I could see the space in Ceri's kitchen where her dog and the basket had been.

"You're lucky your mum is that kind of normal," Ceri said. "She's there for you the way a mother should be."

I grimaced. "Isn't that awful? I've never really thought about it. She's always there." I fought a tear. "Until she wasn't."

Ceri tried to distract me.

"And your dad?"

"Mum holds the family together. Dad plays the fun guy. He's thirty-six, but he acts as if he's fifteen, always cracking jokes and messing around. He's like a firework, fun to watch, but you need to handle with care. I don't think he ever grew up."

I watched the waves rolling in. "He'll be on the way back to the UK by now."

"You reckon?"

"Yes, you can get a red-eye and be in Manchester by dawn." I thought about the phone in my pocket and the battery in Ceri's. Without contact, it felt as if I'd fallen through a hole in the sky and I was in some alternative universe. "Maybe I should call him. Or Otis."

"You said you were going to phone tomorrow."

"It's killing me not knowing anything."

"You wanted it to be tomorrow," Ceri said. "Stick to it."

She'd changed. Back in Liverpool all she ever did was harp on about the police. Out here, she was a different person altogether. I didn't remember her mentioning them once.

"Fine." I fumbled in my pocket for change. "Do you want an ice cream?"

Ceri wrapped herself in her jacket.

"Are you kidding? It's freezing."

"You don't call this freezing, do you? It's a bit windy, that's all. So do you want one or not?"

We walked along the promenade with our ice creams. Finally, we turned back in the direction of the B&B. Ceri tossed Tilly her cone and the Labrador munched away happily.

"It'll be good to get back to my room," Ceri said. "I just want somewhere to relax. I need to feel safe."

Maybe that's what growing up is all about. It's that moment you hear Bob Marley tell you everything's going to be all right and you know it's just a song.

Still, Ceri needed me to be there for her so I told her what she needed to hear. "Safe is good."

At the corner of Mrs Jones's road, Tilly slowed. The hair rose on her back.

"What's up with her?" Ceri wondered out loud.

I hesitated, a sense of apprehension growing inside me.

"Something wrong?" Ceri asked.

"I don't know. She senses something."

My gaze strayed along the road. Things were happening nightmare-slow. It was the way it is in movies, when some unspoken danger bleeds into the corner of the shot. The road pitched and darkness bubbled around the edge of my vision. I trusted the dog's instincts. Something was wrong, but I still couldn't place it. There were a couple of kids kicking a ball around, a guy vacuuming the inside of his car – a green VW hatchback – the usual line of parked vehicles. There was a little girl playing in the yard. It was such an ordinary scene. What was wrong? That's when I saw it. Mrs Jones had one of the upstairs windows open. She seemed to be poking something through. Her movements were rushed, made clumsy by haste.

"What's she doing?"

Ceri followed my stare.

"She's messing with her curtains. What's the big deal? She's only cleaning."

I felt the pulse thump in my throat.

"That's not it. Ceri, that's not it at all. We have to get out of here."

Just then, a gust caught the material and it fluttered out into the wind. It all seemed to happen in slow motion, the bright material rippling against the afternoon sky. Tilly started to bark. Now I knew.

"No. Oh no."

Ceri frowned. "What's wrong?"

"That song, the one about the yellow ribbon. Bethan's trying to warn us."

Simultaneously, a car door opened. I saw the guy emerging from the black four-by-four. Ceri screamed.

"It's Fat Lad!"

I searched for a way out.

Too slow.

Too late.

What I saw next made my insides melt. Snakehead was racing towards us from the opposite direction. Clown to the left of me, joker to the right. Only Snakehead was neither. He was a monster.

"Run!"

Ceri was on her toes in an instant, Tilly racing ahead of her. I tried to set off after them, but a powerful hand seized my wrist, crushing my arm and swinging me round roughly so I stumbled. My ankle gave way for a moment and I felt a stab of pain. My shoes were skidding on the pavement. There was a menacing, fleshless face in front of me and I knew it was over. Snakehead was snarling at me.

"You've caused us a lot of problems."

I tried to struggle free, clawing at the vice-like grip.

Snakehead looked up. "Tommo, give me a hand here."

Fat Lad came running. For the first time, one of them had a name. Up to that point, they hadn't been men. They had been attack dogs, anonymous figures that appeared from nowhere. I was trying to shake myself free, but Snakehead was too strong. I gazed in despair down the street.

"Looking for the Lincoln?" Snakehead chuckled. "Wondering why you didn't spot us earlier?"

I noticed a detail. He had a scarf round his neck, disguising his tattoo.

"Way ahead of you. I decided it was too much of a giveaway and swapped cars. Got you there, didn't I?" He shook me until my teeth rattled. "Got something to say, smart-arse?" Another shake. "Want to flip me the finger now? Not so brave when you're collared, are you?"

"Get off me!"

Fat Lad grabbed my other arm. The sour smell of sweat was overwhelming. Mrs Jones was at the door, bundling Tilly indoors and watching the scene with anxious eyes. She had hold of her phone. Ceri was halfway down the street. She stopped to look back.

"Keep running, Ceri. Get away!"

"She won't get far," Snakehead said. "It hardly matters anyway. We've got what we came for." He wrestled the camera off me. "Let's have a look at the photos. Without evidence, you've got nothing."

Fat Lad took over, pinning my arms. As Snakehead took the camera from its case, I was aware of the guy vacuuming his car. He'd stopped what he was doing and he was watching. The driver's side door was open. He pushed the vacuum cleaner away and took a step forward.

"Hey, what's going on here?"

"Nothing to see, mate," Snakehead said. "He's my nephew. Right little sod. Kicks off for nothing. His mum is worried sick. I'm taking him home." A purposeful nod at the car. "Get on with what you're doing."

His voice carried an unspoken threat, but the man wasn't impressed. He took another step, hesitant, but prepared to make a stand.

"I think you should let that kid go."

Snakehead jabbed a finger. "I told you, he's my nephew."

The guy didn't believe a word. "So let him tell me that. Look, I want you to let him go."

Snakehead didn't like being told what to do. "And I want you to shut your fat mouth before I shut it for you."

"You don't frighten me," the man said, not entirely convincingly. "Let the boy go."

I found my voice. "Don't believe him. He isn't my uncle."

"That does it," the car-cleaner said. "I'm phoning the police."

Snakehead forced a cold grin. "You don't want to do that." He eyeballed the guy. "Something they don't tell you about heroes. They get hurt."

"Are you threatening me?"

This was my chance. Taking advantage of the argument, I managed to squirm loose. I slammed into Snakehead, throwing him off balance. The camera flew from his grasp and hit the pavement. I heard the casing crack. There were other sounds. I took advantage of the moment to drive my foot into Fat Lad's shin. He squealed like a stuck pig. Then there was somebody else in the mix. It was Mrs Jones, laying into Fat Lad with Tilly's lead, slashing him across the temple. In the blur of confusion, an engine roared, tyres screamed then Ceri's face appeared. She was at the wheel of the hatchback.

"Get in!"

Snakehead had hold of my jacket, but something was distracting him too. While he still had one eye on the car-cleaner, Tilly locked her jaws on his trouser leg and pulled with all her might. One moment of hope was all I needed. I tore at the zip and wriggled out of the sleeves. I lost the jacket and Snakehead stumbled backwards, sprawling over Fat Lad's foot. I threw myself into the car. Ceri accelerated away with my legs still hanging out.

"Go, go!" I scrambled inside and pulled at the door.

"There's one more thing." Ceri hit the brakes and slapped a screwdriver in my palm. "Do their tyres."

Fat Lad pushed Mrs Jones away so that she stumbled against a garden gate. Snakehead was still trying to get Tilly to let go of his trouser leg. Car-wash guy was standing by an empty space where the vehicle had been, hands on head. It would be a while before he left his keys in the ignition again.

"Are you kidding?" I cried.

"Do you want them following us?"

I twisted round, jumped out and made for the four-by-four. My legs were like jelly. "Make sure you don't stall the car."

"Don't worry about me. You do the tyres. I'll do the driving."

I jabbed the screwdriver at the front passenger-side tyre. There was a satisfying thump as it sank in. I was going to do another tyre, but Snakehead was almost on top of me. I flung myself back into the passenger seat.

"Go, go, go!"

There were no more words as Ceri hit the gas. Flailing hands slapped at the back of the vehicle then fell away. Ceri was yelling at the top of her voice and pounding the steering wheel.

"Yaaaaa! Did you see what I did?"

I managed to pull the door shut then twisted round to see the goons vanishing in the distance.

"That was . . . amazing."

Ceri grinned.

"I told you my granddad taught me to drive."

I was seeing her in a new light.

"He didn't teach you to drive like that!"

Ceri's face was flushed with her victory.

"How do you know?"

"Granddads don't watch *2 Fast, 2 Furious*. They watch *Antiques Roadshow*."

"You don't know my granddad."

"Who was he, Vin Diesel?"

Ceri laughed. "We never went over twenty miles an hour. Oh, this is way better than that booze. Pure adrenalin kick."

Her smile faltered as she wondered about Mrs Jones and Tilly.

"What can you see back there?"

I craned my neck.

"They're all right, Ceri. Keep going."

Her eyes glittered with joy. "Did you see their faces? They really thought they had us."

"I was too busy trying to get them off me." I watched the streets flashing by. "I just feel sorry for that guy. One minute he's cleaning his car. The next it's speeding off down the street without him."

Ceri wrinkled her nose.

"He'll get it back." She beat her palms on the steering wheel. "I feel wired."

This was an entirely different Ceri to the frightened kid who'd begged me to phone the police.

"Are you for real? You're enjoying this."

Ceri rocked back and forth in her seat and gave a loud yell.

"You got that right. I'm on fire."

"What's got into you?"

She was bouncing in her seat. "Freedom. Freedom's got into me."

"Try not to do any damage to the car," I said. "That guy did try to help us."

Ceri nodded and hung a left.

"Where are we going?" I asked, still shaky from all the excitement.

"As far from here as we can get. We owe Mrs Jones."

I finally managed to buckle up. "You're not wrong. That was fast thinking."

"Where did the screwdriver come from?"

"Back there."

There was a toolbox on the back seat.

"I wonder what he does for a living."

Ceri shrugged. "He won't be doing much until he gets his car back."

By then, we were on our way out of town.

"So what do we do now?"

"We've got a bit of time," Ceri answered. "They won't be going anywhere."

"Don't be too sure. I only had time to do one tyre."

"They've still got to change it."

"I'm just saying we can't take any chances. They could be right on our tail."

"Yes, but what are the chances? Just chill, will you?"

I did a double take. Suddenly, she was completely in charge. She didn't seem afraid of anything. Well, I was.

"Ceri, listen to me. We need to get off the main road and dump the car. It's stolen. The police will be on the lookout."

Ceri negotiated a roundabout. "Then what?"

I plumped for honesty. "No idea."

"You always make out you're in charge."

"So I'm a fake, OK? I'm scared and I'm expecting to see

those guys coming after us any minute. We still need to get off the road."

Ceri gave the situation some thought. "You could have a point. The theft will have been reported by now."

"Bethan was on the phone when I looked back. I think she was calling the police. She's worried about you."

There was the angry glare again.

"Talk about me, did you?"

"Might have."

It was late afternoon and a few house lights were flickering. I was starting to give some thought to what we were going to do next. We had to get through the next few hours and we had nowhere to stay.

"Right, we're not meant to be back in Liverpool until tomorrow. I'm not trying to be funny, but where do we spend the night? Think it through, Ceri. Once the police talk to Bethan, they're going to be checking all the B&Bs. That option's closed."

I had her attention.

"You still won't talk to the coppers?"

"Not when they've still got Mum and Trinity."

Was that the whole story? Was I really the dutiful son? Maybe I was feeling something of Ceri's hunger for a different life.

It was a few moments before Ceri answered. "We'll have to improvise. What if we pull up somewhere and sleep in the car?"

"When the police are looking for it? It's a bit of a risk, don't you think?"

We joined the A55. There was still no sign of anyone following. I was twitchy as hell, but Ceri was strangely calm.

"Chill, OK?" Ceri said. "I just saved your bacon."

I squeezed her forearm for a second. "Sorry. You're right. I owe you. I didn't think you had it in you. I mean, where did that come from?"

"I have no idea."

After that we fell silent. I twisted in my seat and looked back, searching for some sign of the black four-by-four, the police, anybody.

The road was clear.

Five minutes later there was still no sign of anyone following.

"So how long do we stay on this road?"

Ceri was doing a steady sixty-five. For somebody who'd never driven over twenty before, she was doing OK. I had confidence in her.

"Don't ask me," she said. "I'm all out of ideas."

She looked at the fading light and started to fiddle with the controls.

"How do you put the headlights on?"

I stared in disbelief. "You don't know?"

"I've never had the lights on in a car! It was always daylight when Granddad showed me."

Ceri was still tinkering with the instruments. I didn't like the way she kept taking her eyes off the road. What's the point of giving your pursuers the slip then wrapping yourself round the back of a lorry?

She was starting to get frustrated.

"Oh, how do you put them on? I can make a car go and I can steer. That's it. Oh, I forgot to tell you, I never did reversing either."

I burst out laughing, seriously nervous laughter by this point. I was doing sixty with somebody who knew as much about cars as I knew about brain surgery.

"Reversing's out, then. Just go forward."

Ceri was still fumbling around the dashboard. The car started to drift into the next lane.

"You concentrate on the road. Let me do the lights."

Suddenly there were no more protests.

"OK."

I found the switch, but that didn't solve our problems. Simultaneously, we heard the wail of a siren behind us. I looked back and I could see the blue emergency lights of a cop car behind us. It was coming up fast.

"Get off the road, Ceri."

She stared frantically ahead.

"There's a slip road coming up."

"So take it."

We left the main carriageway and drove up a narrow, winding road that climbed steeply before we spotted a layby. She pulled in and killed the engine.

"Did they go past?"

I nodded.

"They weren't after us."

"Are you sure?"

I shook my head.

"I don't know anything any more, but they're not here, are they?"

Ceri killed the lights and we sat in the evening gloom.

"What now?"

"Beats me. I'm all out of ideas. Maybe we should wait here a while and go back home."

Ceri flipped.

"I'm not going home!"

She was yelling. Instinctively, I reached for her and she flinched.

"I'm not going to hurt you. I'm not your rotten mother . . ." At that moment, I hated myself. I could have bitten my own tongue out. "Ceri, I'm sorry. I would never hurt you."

The wind gusted around us. The last rays of the setting sun faded over the hills.

I was starting to realise how broken up Ceri really was. The wind continued to buffet the car.

I wanted her to trust me. "I care about you."

Ceri saw the way I was reaching for her hands and pulled away.

"John, you've done your best to take care of me. Don't think I'm not grateful. It's just . . ."

"What?"

"I hardly know you. Until we started this project together, we hadn't exchanged a word. You were one face among all the others."

A face in the crowd. Is that all I was?

"Thanks."

"Oh, stop sulking. Don't tell me you're going to throw another wobbler."

"Another one! When did I throw the first one?"

"You're always going off on one."

"No, I'm not."

Ceri stared me out. "You know what I mean. You and me, we're strangers."

We sat for some time in the dark then I put a hand on Ceri's shoulder, just for a moment.

"We're tired. Maybe you're right. Liverpool isn't such a good idea. We lie low until tomorrow morning. It's not like we can use this car. It's stolen. Let's get it out of sight."

Looking back, maybe we could have done things differently. At the time, it seemed the right thing to do.

"The car's risky," Ceri said. "Let's have a look around. If there's no other shelter, we come back to the car. What do you say?"

"I've never done anything like this."

"Me neither."

We trudged up the hill for the best part of an hour. There wasn't a single soul anywhere.

"A bit different to Liverpool."

151

Ceri nodded. "There are no convenience stores for starters. I'm starving."

I glanced up at the troubled sky. "Did you feel rain?"

Ceri glared. "Oh, don't say that. I'm cold. I'm hungry. Getting wet through would be the last straw."

I was starting to wonder what we were doing there. There had been some kind of logic to this thing at first. Now we just seemed to be running for the sake of it. Everything was spinning out of control. Suddenly Ceri stopped.

"Something wrong?"

She pointed. "What's that?"

I peered into the gloom. "I don't see anything."

"There. A hut or something."

"You've got better eyesight than me."

Ceri unlatched the gate opposite and led the way through.

"Where are you going?"

"It could be shelter." She waved her arms. "Or maybe you want to sleep in a ditch."

I was wondering whether the car might be the best option after all. I hung back for a few moments then I followed her, closing the gate behind me. Ceri was right about the shape in the darkness, it was a small stone hut. We poked our heads inside.

"It's a bit whiffy," I observed. "What is that smell?"

"Sheep."

"Come again?"

"It's sheep. They have this oily stuff on their fleece, lanolin."

"So now you're an expert on sheep. You're a sheepologist."

"I read it somewhere. It's sheep all right. Eau de Mutton."

"*Mouton.*"

"What?"

"Sheep in French. It's *mouton.*"

"What's know-all in French?"

She ignored me and looked around. "So what do you think?"

"What do I think about what?"

She started to clear a space for us to sit down. "This. It'll keep out the wind and the rain."

I gave the place the once-over. I wasn't impressed. "You mean we're going to sleep *here*?"

Ceri was kicking debris around. "Have you got a better idea? You said yourself, the police will be looking for the car."

I peered at the floor. It would take forever to clear a space big enough to sleep. "It's manky."

"Beggars can't be choosers." Ceri sat with her back against the wall. "It's better than nothing."

I joined her and chuckled. "Have you seen the state of your shoes?"

Ceri pulled one off. She waggled it and the sole flapped like the mouth of a puppet. "I know, the sole is coming away from the upper. They weren't made for hiking up mountains."

I sniffed at my armpits. "I'd kill for a shower."

That's the trouble with dreams. You wake up. And I was feeling grubby.

Ceri ran her tongue over her teeth. "I'd kill for a toothbrush. Where's the camera?"

"Smashed. I lost hold of it in the struggle."

Ceri's eyes widened. "So we don't have any proof they killed that guy?"

At least I'd done something right. I produced the memory card. "I've got it here."

Ceri was impressed. "You took it out of the camera? You kept it safe."

"Yes, I'm not sure why. It made sense at the time."

Ceri gave me a hug. "You're not so stupid, after all."

"Thanks." I replayed her words. "Hey, when did you think I was stupid?"

Ceri giggled and put her hand to her mouth. "Oops."

I'm not sure I was really angry, but I made my half-hearted protest. "Why am I stupid?"

"You're not. I'm just teasing."

I watched her for a moment. I could have gazed into her hazel eyes for ever. Ceri seemed to read my thoughts and looked away. That's how it was. The moment we started to get close, she always shied off.

"So how do we do this?" she said. "I'm not lying down

among all this crap. Have you seen the state of the floor? Besides, there could be bugs."

Eventually, we settled for trying to sleep sitting up, backs leaning against the wall. We listened to the rush of the wind outside.

"We'll have to find somewhere to get a wash in the morning," Ceri said.

"Chance would be a fine thing. These huts aren't en suite. We're in the middle of nowhere."

"They've got to have services on the A55."

"Yes, but the nearest one could be miles off. We might be walking for hours."

"Hitch-hike?"

That sounded like a really bad idea.

"The police are going to be on the lookout after yesterday. Then there's Itchy and Scratchy. Forgotten about them? We've got proof they murdered a guy. They're not going to give up."

"Well, we can't just stay here."

We turned our options over for a few minutes, but we were no wiser at the end of our conversation. It all seemed so hopeless. The dream had turned into grubby reality.

"We should sleep on it," I said.

It was easier said than done, at least for me. Ceri fell asleep quickly, head resting on my shoulder. I liked the feel of her against me. It was a protective thing. After a while, I slipped an arm around her. To be honest, I was too tired to make a move on her. I was glad of the warmth. I'd had to abandon my jacket on the road outside the B&B. It felt as if I was shedding everything I owned, item by item. I had no coat, no laptop, no camera. To be honest, I didn't have much of anything any more.

Including parents.

All I had was Ceri.

She didn't even register my arm. She was already in a deep sleep. It was weird that I didn't feel more resentment towards her. What was it like, being alone in the world the way she was? I saw into the long, deep darkness she must face every day and I squeezed her shoulders gently.

Ceri slept on.

I woke to see the light of a watery, greyish dawn spreading across the floor. I stared down at my stockinged feet and wriggled my toes. You'd think I would be depressed after everything that had happened, but I was glad to be alive. One of my shoes was lying on its side. Ceri had said something about bugs so I righted it carefully. I would have to shake them out in any case. I thought about the way Ceri had flipped on me. What had I said to upset her? I was still turning it over in my mind when I heard the noise. There it was again, a steady, rhythmic thump.

Footsteps.

I stiffened. Images of Snakehead and Fat Lad stuttered through my mind. I tried to ease Ceri away from me so I could find a weapon. She must have sensed the movement and looked up. Her cheek was creased where she'd been lying against me.

"What's wrong?"

"Listen." There it was again. "There's somebody out there."

Ceri had that startled look in her eyes again.

"Police?"

She hoped it was the police. The alternative was too awful to consider.

"I don't know."

There was part of a rotting window frame by the wall. I armed myself with it and pressed a finger to my lips. The footsteps were coming closer. Ceri's fingernails dug into my arm. Any other time, I would have been enjoying the attention, but all I could think about was looking straight into Snakehead's pale, almost colourless eyes. The guy was a psycho. He didn't just hurt people for money. He liked it. What had made us think we could get away? They were remorseless, hounds from hell.

"What do we do?" she whispered.

There was one way in and one way out. The stone hut didn't even have a window. I was too scared to answer. That's when a shadowy form appeared in the doorway and I relaxed.

"Another rotten sheep! What is it with Wales and sheep?"

Ceri burst out laughing.

"Who's afraid of the big, bad sheep, the big, bad sheep, the big, bad sheep?"

"You were scared too." I waved at the stupid animal. "Shoo."

Ceri was rocking with laughter.

"Who's afraid of the big bad sheep? Baa baa baa baa baa."

I waved my arms again. "Shoo, you dumb sheep."

She howled derision at my clumsy attempt to chase the beast away

"Shoo?" she snorted derisively.

"Well, you tell me how to get rid of a sheep and I'll say it."

"What about mint sauce?"

"Ha ha."

The sheep watched with its flat face and strange, elongated pupils. I got up and windmilled my arms furiously.

"Mint sauce! Mint sauce!"

The sheep was backing off. Only slowly. I spun round and punched the air in triumph.

"I fought the sheep and I won."

Ceri was squealing with laughter. Suddenly I felt a thump in my buttocks and pitched forward. The sheep had just nudged me in the backside with its head. Ceri was now screaming even louder.

"He butted you in the arse. John fought the sheep and the sheep won."

That did it. I chased the sheep up the hillside, watching the way it bobbed along in front of me. When I returned from my pursuit Ceri was almost in tears. I liked the way she laughed.

"Oh, that was brilliant," she said, eyes sparkling.

So I did something I'd been meaning to do for two days. I leaned forward and kissed her. The time seemed so right, but her reaction was so wrong. She pulled away, shoved me roughly and stamped out of the hut. When I tried to follow, she turned and screamed at me.

"Leave me alone!"

"But . . ."

"What kind of creep are you?"

I had no answer.

"Don't you ever do that again! Don't you dare try to take advantage of me!"

I felt a hot rush down my spine. I'd meant it to be beautiful and she'd turned it into something grubby.

"I'm sorry. We were having fun. I thought . . ."

Ceri ran at me, shoving at my chest. "You thought what? You thought what exactly, that I was easy? Poor Ceri, she's all alone so I can do what I like. What is it with guys? They think they can paw you any time they want."

That wasn't it at all. Why was she acting like this?

"It was just a kiss, a spur of the moment thing. I . . ."

My eyes were stinging. How had it gone so wrong?

"Oh, now you're feeling sorry for yourself. Well, don't. I'm the one with the crappy, stinking life here."

Something inside me snapped. You want to play the

victim, Ceri James? Well, tough, I've got just as many misery points in the bank of bum deals.

"You want to play this game? I'll see you your junkie of a mother and raise you a kidnap. Forgotten that, have you? My mum and sister could be anywhere. They could be . . ."

I didn't even want to say it. We stood, staring at each other. We were both out of breath.

"OK," Ceri said, recovering herself. "I'll forget it this one time, but don't do it again. Got it?"

I wasn't ready to take a lecture.

"Oh, I've got it, all right. One minute, you're all over me, the next you don't want to know."

Ceri stared in disbelief. "When was I all over you?"

"You threw your arms around me last night or have you forgotten? You slept with your head on my shoulder. What else am I supposed to think?"

Ceri's eyes were hard. "I was hugging you as a friend. What, I fancied you in my sleep, did I? I didn't even know I had my head on your shoulder, that's how tired I was. Don't start imagining something that isn't there."

We glared at each other for another few moments then Ceri turned. "Do you hear that?"

"What?"

Her temper had ebbed as quickly as it had risen.

"It's water. There's a stream."

She retrieved her battered shoes and led the way across the slope. You'd think we hadn't even had an argument. I trudged after her, burning with resentment. There was a clear stream, flowing over stones.

"Do you think it's clean, you know, drinkable?"

I was still stinging from the rejection. "Try it. With any luck, it's poisoned. Strychnine might do something for your lousy temper."

"Oh, grow up," she snapped. "Only little kids sulk."

She really knew how to get under my skin. "I'm not sulking!"

"Could have fooled me."

She tucked her hair behind her ears and cupped the cold, fresh water. She tasted it, waited a beat then gulped a few mouthfuls. She proceeded to splash her face and wipe it on her sleeve.

"It's good. You should try it."

I deadpanned. It didn't get the reaction I was planning. Ceri cupped water from the stream in her hands and threw it all over me.

"You splashed me!"

"You deserved it."

I splashed her back. She retaliated. Within moments we were in the middle of a water fight. It wasn't long before I was getting the best of it.

"That's not fair. You've got bigger hands than me."

I cupped my hands and threw more.

"OK," she said. "Truce."

I stared her down for a moment then I drank and washed my face.

"Better?" Ceri asked.

I kept blanking her so she gave me a shove. There was nothing to grab on to so I found myself sitting in the shallow stream. I was soaked right through to my underpants. I struggled out and yelled at her.

"Are you crazy? What was that for?"

She was laughing.

"For being such a moron." The laughter stopped. "I'm not looking for a relationship, OK?"

"Fine." I felt my trousers. "Great, I'm soaked." Then I remembered something. "Oh no. Oh, crap!"

"What?"

"I've got my phone in my pocket. Look at it. It's waterlogged."

"Try the battery."

She handed it over. I slotted it in and tried to switch the phone on. Nothing.

"It's dead. Now I can't even make my call."

"You know what to do when a phone goes in water?"

"I'm sure you're going to enlighten me."

She did. "You put it in rice. I saw it on YouTube."

Ceri had come out with some corkers, but this was the best yet. I gestured at the bleak hillside.

"So where are we going to get rice then? I don't see a convenience store. Maybe there's a Chinese takeaway on the other side of the rocks." I made my way over. "No, just more rocks."

Ceri folded her arms. "There's no need to be sarcastic."

162

"There's every need to be sarcastic." I examined the memory card from the camera. "This is probably ruined too. That's our evidence gone."

"Sorry," she said.

Sorry? That was it?

"You should be," I snarled. "That's really dropped us in it. You're off your head, you are. What did you have to shove me for?"

"You were acting like a creep. You don't come on to a girl when she isn't showing any interest."

"I thought you *were* interested."

"Don't flatter yourself. I'm not."

I folded my arms. "So I see."

My neck was burning with humiliation. What was wrong with me? What was wrong with *her*? I took a look at the mountain: the sheep-dotted slopes, the few trees clinging to the hillside, the stone walls. This was just great. We were in the middle of nowhere and we were all out of luck: no memory card, no phone. I didn't even have my lousy jacket to keep me warm.

"We don't even have any proof those guys did anything. There goes our only bargaining counter. Mum and Trinity are depending on me. This just gets better and better."

It was a while before I spoke again.

"Good job I kept the money in my shirt pocket." I pulled out the folding stuff. "At least we can get something to eat."

Ceri gestured at the empty landscape. "The question is where."

I saw the sheep that had butted me, well, a sheep that looked like the one that had butted me. Sheep all look the same to a city boy.

"Yahhhh!"

"Don't take it out on the sheep, you big bully."

Just to spite her, I set off after it, yelling at the top of my voice. "Yahhh!"

Bad move. I had just attracted unwanted attention. A Land Rover screeched to a halt and a guy in a green, quilted body warmer, wellington boots and cap got out.

"What do you think you're doing? Get out of that field."

I swapped glances with Ceri. We walked to the road like guilty kids.

"Have you got no sense?" the farmer demanded.

Ceri glared at me. "*He* hasn't."

The farmer heard the accent and shoved his cap back with his thumb.

"You're not from round here, are you?"

"Sharp, aren't you?"

"Liverpool?"

Well, duh.

"Yes."

He looked around. "Parents with you?"

I jumped in before Ceri could make him suspicious. "Yes, they're back at the B&B."

"Which B&B is that?"

"Llan-something. Llandiddlydoodah. Over there."

Good thinking. To a Scouser, everything in Wales is Llan-something. I waved vaguely. The farmer was still curious.

"You don't look much like brother and sister."

"She's my cousin."

"Cousin, eh?"

Ceri chipped in. "Yes, I'm his cousin." She sniffed. "Worst luck."

Old MacDonald smiled. "You'd better be going, then. It looks like rain."

We trudged away. We were so wet, rain wouldn't make much difference. The farmer watched us go.

Maybe he watched us with a bit too much interest.

Old MacDonald was right about the rain.

Here it came, fat, cold drops thudding on our faces, drumming on the ground, oozing off the leaves. It came in silvery sheets, drifting across the landscape, suddenly made wintry by the downpour. OK, I was wrong. It did make a difference. Now we weren't just wet. We were cold. We walked in silence. I was shivering in my thin shirt. I really missed that jacket. Another reason to hate Snakehead. I imagined him going through the pockets, rummaging for the memory card before cursing and wishing me dead. Did I leave anything behind, anything that could help him, notes, receipts, tickets? I couldn't think. There's nothing like fear for wiping the memory banks.

So another stage in our journey began. Ceri squelched along in her wrecked shoes. She had a face like a storm cloud. I'd messed up big style with that stupid kiss and she wasn't going to let me forget it. We retraced our steps down the hillside. The rain started to come down harder. Ceri blinked at the sky, lashes bright with raindrops.

"We're going to get drenched."

"Drenchder."

"That isn't even a word!"

And she wasn't even a companion. We were reaching the stage when we could quite easily loathe each other.

"The car isn't far. We could shelter inside until the shower goes off."

"Bit of a risk, isn't it? What about the coppers?"

I gestured at the leaden sky. "Do you want to stay out in this lot?"

Ceri nodded. "Car it is."

But there was to be no shelter from the downpour. We were turning a corner when Ceri tugged at my sleeve and spat out an urgent warning.

"Police!"

The word sent a rush of adrenalin through me. She dragged me into the bracken, shoving at my head as if I was a stubborn dog. Police. The word crackled through me like electricity. We crouched in the dripping undergrowth, watching the scene. My heart was slamming as I peered out at the cops. One car. Two officers, one male, one female. The guy was leaning into the VW, poking around. The woman was talking into her radio. We retreated into the woods to our left and peered down the lane.

"What do we do now?" Ceri hissed.

I could have laughed at the turnaround. What had happened to the Ceri who'd spent the day before demanding I phone 999?

"Well, you wanted to go to the police," I said. "Here's your chance." I held out my hand. "Go on, knock yourself out."

"What about your family?"

I ignored her and kept a stony face.

"Oh, you're not sulking again!"

"I'm cold. I'm wet. I don't have a clue what's going on. The fate of my family is a mystery. What's not to like?"

She glared. "Stop feeling sorry for yourself."

"Look who's talking." My voice was raised. I checked that the police hadn't heard, then lowered it. "Wah, my mum's a druggie. My gran's dying. My life's so crap. Boo hoo."

Oh, that was really clever. What was wrong with me? I hated the sound of my own voice. Why did I have to be so cruel? Ceri didn't rise to it. She was tougher than I thought.

"Keep talking like that and you'll be making your way back to Liverpool alone. Now cut it out and tell me what you want."

"No, tell me what *you* want because I don't know any more."

Ceri scowled. "I want to run and keep on running. I don't want to go back ever. OK, that's my contribution. Other than that, I'm all out of ideas. Now it's your turn, Einstein."

I watched the police searching the vehicle. "My dad said no bizzies. Otis said stay under the radar. We stay here until they've gone."

Ceri wiped the rain from her face. "So we stay on the run. Works for me."

"What's happened to you, Ceri James? You wouldn't stop going on about the coppers. They're right there."

"You don't want to involve them. Those gangsters will hurt your mum and sister."

Her concern didn't ring true.

"This isn't about me, though, is it?"

Ceri blinked away the rain. "No, you're right. It isn't."

"So what?"

Her face lit with a kind of madness.

"I'm not going back to Greenways."

"I thought you said it was OK."

"I said I could put up with it, but no, it's not OK. Nothing's OK."

I didn't know what to make of this outburst.

"What then?"

"The people who take care of me are lovely, but they're not family. It isn't *home*."

We were two lost souls without a home.

"So where is?"

"My nan's. Bethan's. Anywhere where somebody gives a damn about me. Not Greenways. It's . . . an *institution*."

But her nan was ill and Bethan couldn't help. They were both out of bounds. Ceri was standing in the woods, under the dripping leaves, drenched to the skin, and she thought it was better than going back to Liverpool. Anything was better than that. She looked at me.

"You're trembling."

"I'm freezing. It's all this rotten rain."

Ceri stared at the sky. The clouds were parting and soft light filled the sky.

"I think it's stopping."

Then she did something surprising. She unzipped her coat and wrapped it and herself around me the best she could. I swear, I didn't know what to make of Ceri James. I had the same desire to kiss her, but I knew better than to try. Last time went well. We must have stood there like that for four, five minutes, silent, kind of confused, what some psychologist geek might call bonding, then Ceri pulled away.

"Listen?"

The police car was leaving, followed by a truck towing the VW.

"Let's go," Ceri said.

She had only taken a couple of steps when her feet stuck in the mud. She pulled off her right shoe and showed it to me. The sole had almost completely detached.

"They're finished."

She removed the left shoe as well and threw the ruined pair into the trees. She padded away in bare feet.

"Coming?"

By the time we reached the services, I was carrying her piggyback. There was nothing chivalrous about it. She just wouldn't stop yelping as she stumbled over the chippings so I decided to do mule service.

"Do you have to keep making that noise?" I snapped.

"I'm not doing it on purpose," she growled. "My feet are cut to shreds."

So I carried her. She wasn't that heavy. She thought it was really funny and gave me giddyups all the way. I was forgiven for the attempted kiss. It took us an hour's walk, maybe a little more to cover the distance. All the time, I felt as if Snakehead would pull up as we plodded along the hard shoulder. I must have carried her about a quarter of the way, taking breaks when she got too heavy, or am I exaggerating? Everybody likes to play the hero. When we got there, the café looked well-lit and inviting.

"Civilisation at last," I grunted.

Ceri patted me on the back like a good donkey.

"Order me something. I'm going to wash my feet. They're destroyed."

Her feet were tiny, very red and caked with mud. There were one or two scratches.

"I look stupid enough with no shoes. At least I can make sure they're clean."

"What do you want?"

"Bacon sandwich. No, make that two. I'm starving. And a coffee." She got to the door. "And something sweet."

"Looks like Otis has given you a taste for coffee."

Ceri shook her head. "Not really. Right now I'd drink anything that would warm me through."

I ordered four sandwiches, two bacon for Ceri, two sausage for me. There were muffins so I added them to the tray. I'd already eaten the first sandwich by the time she emerged from the toilet. She slid into the booth sharpish, keen not to have her feet noticed. There was an elderly couple by the window, a lorry driver in a hi-vis jacket to our right. Ceri devoured the first sandwich. She seemed distracted.

"Are you OK?"

"I'm fine."

She didn't sound fine.

"Could you pass me a tissue?"

I handed her one. "You've quit bitching at me then?"

She stiffened. "Don't use that word."

I waited for an explanation.

"Mum's men used to call her a bitch when they were slapping her round our flat. Nobody's ever going to say that to me."

This was the first time she had opened a window into her home life.

"I didn't strictly say it *to* you."

"I know, but I hate the word. It's poison."

"You said it yourself. You said it about your mum."

Ceri dropped her eyes. "I did, didn't I?"

She turned and stared at the lorry driver. I ran my gaze over the café. Nobody was paying us any attention. The staff weren't much older than us. One was local. The other had a Polish accent. Or was it Latvian? They seemed bored, as if they wanted to be somewhere else. Maybe that's how the whole world was, wishing it was somewhere else. The elderly man and woman were laughing about something. The driver had his nose buried in a newspaper. Ceri still had eyes on him.

"You keep staring at that guy," I said. "What gives?"

"He's a creep."

I laughed. "Bit of a value judgement. I'm sure he's OK if you get to know him."

She crossed her arms. "You don't understand."

"Well, I can't if you don't tell me anything."

She whispered the explanation. "He touched me up as I went past."

Suddenly I saw the guy differently. "You're kidding!"

She stared me out. "What, you think I'd make something like that up?

I watched him reading his newspaper, calm as anything.

"I should set fire to that stinking rag," I grunted. "Look what he's reading. Murdoch's lousy scandal sheet."

She nodded. "You want to? Do it. I dare you."

"What?"

"I dare you to burn it."

Suddenly I wasn't feeling quite so brave.

"I don't have a match."

Ceri was sounding excited. "I'll get you one."

"You're crazy."

She laughed. "And you're all talk."

Ceri went over to the old couple. She was back a few moments later with a lighter. What had I talked myself into?

"Go on, then."

"You're nuts."

"You said that." She made with the hard eyes, daring me. "See, you're a coward."

A minibus had just pulled in at the petrol station opposite. A guy in a leather jacket started to fill up. He had dreads. White guy with coffee-coloured dreads. I saw these people in town sometimes, hanging round Church Street in a group. I tore my eyes away from him, the second guy with dreads in my story.

"I'm no coward."

"So do it." She turned away. "Bottler."

My heart was thumping. We were supposed to be keeping our heads low and here she was egging me on to set a paper alight. I came to a decision. Bottler, was I?

"Finished your breakfast?"

"Yes."

"OK, get ready to run."

"You won't do it."

"Watch me."

I went over to the driver and stood in front of him, feet planted apart, kind of provocative. He looked up from his newspaper. I was past the point of no return.

He stared me down with cold, piggy eyes. He was still eyeballing me when the paper caught fire. Oh, it was beautiful. It went up like a torch. Chair legs scraped as he leapt backwards. Simultaneously, Ceri ran squealing through the door. I followed, tossing the lighter to the startled couple by the window.

"You maniac!" the driver yelled, beating out the flames.

Dread Guy Two was returning to the van. He saw us running. On impulse, I shouted a question.

"Can you give us a lift?"

He seemed uncertain.

"We wouldn't ask, but it's an emergency. See that weirdo over there? He tried to touch up my cousin."

Quick thinking. I could have hugged myself. Dread Guy Two looked past me at the driver stumbling through the door to the café. To my surprise, our saviour slid back the rear door.

"Get in." He glared at the driver. "You should be ashamed of yourself, you dirty old man."

The driver yelled something as we bundled into the van. We were already picking up speed on the slip road by the time he gave up the chase and stood wheezing in the car park. Ceri jabbed me in the ribs.

"You mad head! I never thought you'd do it."

I stared down the road and burst out laughing. "Me neither." I roared at the top of my voice. "I burned his paper. Aaaaargh!"

Dread Guy Two ran through the introductions.

"I'm Mop."

"Mop?"

He fiddled with his dreads. "My dad says this is a right mop. So Mop."

There were two other guys, Paul and Bunny and two women, one about our age, the other a little older, Sarah and Freya.

"Goddess of war," I said.

Listen to me. Something at school did go in. Freya turned vivid blue eyes on me. She lived up to her name, tall, striking and in possession of a beautiful, hawkish face framed by tumbling blond hair. Sarah was a slightly older copy.

"Sisters?" I asked.

"I'm sixteen," Freya said. "Sarah's nineteen."

"I like your name," Ceri said. "I wish I was tall like you too." She gestured towards me. "He calls me a Munchkin."

I snorted. "It was dwarf, actually. You could be an Oompa-Loompa."

Freya ignored our verbal fencing.

"Weird combination, isn't it?" she said. "Freya was the goddess of sex and death."

175

"Oh, I don't know," I countered. "Some people say that's what life is all about."

Freya sized us up, dwelling on Ceri's bare feet. "What happened to your shoes?"

"They fell apart."

"How long have you been walking?"

"Hours."

"Where are you going?"

I beat Ceri to the reply. She was liable to get us in more trouble.

"Home. Liverpool. Are you going that far?"

"You're in luck."

The questions kept coming.

"Why was that guy chasing you?"

Ceri did the talking.

"He grabbed my bum."

"Sexist scumbag. Shouldn't you be chasing him?"

Ceri laughed. "John set fire to his paper . . . while he was still reading it."

I saw the eyes turning. Instant respect.

"You never!"

I was enjoying the attention.

"So Ceri's your cousin," Mop said, without taking his eyes off the road.

I decided I might as well own up.

"No, we're friends. I just say that to stop people asking questions."

"So you're together?" Freya asked.

"You're messing, aren't you?" Ceri answered. "Like he said, we're friends. Just friends."

I thought I was a hero for burning that guy's paper. Didn't that earn me some brownie points?

Ceri rubbed at her legs a little self-consciously. "Where are you going?"

"Some of our friends have set up a homeless camp," Freya said. "We're going to support them. There's a march on Saturday."

Saturday. It occurred to me that I'd lost track of the day.

"So you're political?" I asked.

"You could say that. Small *p*. We're not into parties."

"Why not?"

"Hierarchies." Freya started to sing. "You don't own me."

"So what are you into?"

Freya spoke for the others. "Paul, Bunny and Sarah are Sabs."

"Come again?"

"Hunt saboteurs. They disrupt the rich parasites' fun. My parents won't let me go until I'm eighteen."

"You're here."

Sarah laughed. "We're supposed to be having a sleepover at a friend's house. Mum would kill us if she knew."

Freya had this slightly superior smile. I found her unsettling.

"I'm a feminist, anti-fascist, anti-capitalist."

I grunted. "Oh, a rebel with a lot of causes, huh?"

She chuckled. "Right."

"What about you, Mop?"

He took a hand off the wheel and stuck a fist in the air. "Power to the people."

Then he burst out laughing. "I'm just the driver."

I didn't know what to make of his answer. I wondered if he and Freya were together. I had never met people like this.

"I went on a demo once."

"Yes? What was the cause?"

"Black Lives Matter. I was hanging round town with my mates and all these protestors went past."

Freya tried to look interested then started quizzing us again.

"Travel light, don't you?"

Ceri glanced at me, hoping I had an answer. I tried to think of something, couldn't and grunted a single word. "Yes."

"Going home?"

"Kind of."

"Meaning?"

How was I supposed to reply? "It's complicated."

"Leave them alone," Mop said. "They don't owe us an explanation. We're giving them a lift. We don't own them."

I gave him a grateful smile.

"So where are you going now?" Ceri said. "Are you staying overnight somewhere?"

Freya tilted her head. "We're dossing at somebody's flat, having a bit of a party before the demo. That's the idea."

"So we can hang around there until we're picked up. There won't be any trouble."

That was Ceri's promise.

She didn't keep it.

BACK

We were back in Liverpool and I had a call to make.

The thought of it made my stomach turn over. I wanted news, but not if it was bad.

"Can I borrow somebody's phone?" I asked. "Mine got wrecked." Then, as an afterthought, I said: "I'll pay."

A voice came out of the crowd. "No need. You can use mine."

I looked around the room. We were in one of those big, three-storey houses that must have been posh once then got turned into student or young professionals' flats. Mop was the one offering. He was sharing the settee with the guy who let us in, a studenty type called Gummy.

"Why Gummy?"

He grinned and I saw a space where a tooth should be. Ask a stupid question. The flat was spacious, with a high ceiling. There wasn't much furniture. The walls were white. There were a few spidery cracks meandering across the plasterwork. There was no shade on the light bulb.

It was how I imagined the room where Snakehead was holding Mum and Trinity. Mop saw me looking around.

"Yes, it's a bit basic." He slapped Gummy on the shoulder. "But it's home, yeah?"

Gummy agreed. "Yeah."

They started to wrestle around.

"I don't want to interrupt your fun," I said, "but the phone?"

"Oh, right. Here you go."

Mop slapped the phone in my hand and carried on talking. It was the first one I'd used in a while that didn't have the internet. I stepped out on to the landing. Somebody was lugging a speaker up the stairs for the party later in the evening. I sidestepped him and heard footsteps behind me. The slap of flip-flops announced Ceri. It was the only footwear anybody could find for her.

"What are you doing?"

"Calling Jimmy."

I saw the look on her face.

"We said we'd call as soon as we got back," I reminded her.

She said nothing.

"What gives, Ceri? We can't hide for ever."

She rested her back against the wall.

"I don't want to go back."

"We are back."

She let her head drop. "I don't want to go back in that home."

"It's time to break radio silence. What if there have been developments?"

She nodded. Reluctantly. The phone rang three times before anybody picked up.

"It's me."

"Where the hell have you been?"

Jimmy's voice was angry, which was a novelty. He was usually the most laid-back character you could meet.

"That's a nice welcome," I told him.

"What do you expect? You've been driving everybody crazy. Otis said drop under the radar. Temporarily. Not vanish off the face of the earth. So where have you been? What have you been doing?"

What was with the third degree? I thought we'd agreed to this. I rolled events through my mind. Maybe Jimmy had a point.

"I've been keeping my head low the way Otis said."

"There's low and there's disappearing through a black hole. You've had everybody crawling the walls here."

"What, you think it's been easy for me?"

Jimmy took a breath. An anger gap. "Your dad's here."

I heard the familiar voice. It had been a while. Dad opted for calm and practical, at least for the moment. I could hear the fury underneath. The first time we met was going to be fun.

"John. Where are you?"

"Not sure," I said. "We're not far from the city centre. I'll get the address in a minute. I'm safe. I'm with good people."

183

He didn't sound reassured. "Who?"

I couldn't think of a word for what they were.

"Hippies," I said. "No, I mean, kind of alternative."

Dad started to get hostile. "Druggies?"

That was rich, with his history.

"No way." The big question followed, the one I hardly dared ask. "What about Mum, Trinity?"

Dad sounded tense. "They're OK. We've talked over the phone. "

"So they're not home?"

The tension showed in Dad's voice.

"No, our friends want that memory card before they'll let them go."

"Dad, this is bad. They killed a man."

He lowered his voice. "John, I know this is hard for you. I'm trying to sort it."

"The guy on the beach had your number. What's going on?"

"John, I know about Leroy." There was a long pause while he considered his words. "Look, we can't do this over the phone. The police are all over me like a rash. I don't know who's listening in on us."

"The line's tapped?"

"Probably not, but don't say another word. You didn't think the coppers would be involved? Seriously?"

Things started falling in place, like tumblers in a locking system. I would have to watch my words.

"So you've told them everything?" I asked.

"Not everything. There were some questions. Why did it take so long to report you missing? The care home was in touch with them immediately, reporting Ceri's disappearance. We weren't. They were suspicious." He waited a beat then asked me a question. "How the hell have you stayed out of sight so long? It's been on the news."

"Yeah?"

In a weird way, that gave me a kind of buzz.

"Yes. You and this Ceri girl. It was the social services that got the police involved in the first place. Normally, it would be a while before there was any publicity, but there was a killing."

Dad's voice went quiet. He was talking to somebody.

"Dad?"

"I'm with Otis. We don't know how to play this. These are bad people. They keep going on about this memory card."

The image was back in my head. Snakehead with his arm outstretched. Snakehead killing a man. Then the question I was dreading:

"Have you got it?"

Ceri looked at me, mouthed something. The word *no*. She wanted me to stay shtum.

"Dad, it's destroyed."

Ceri rolled her eyes.

"Dad?"

"That was our bargaining counter to get your mum and Trinity back. Did you destroy it?"

"Are you kidding? Why would I? No, it happened by accident."

I could hear his breathing down the phone.

"Do these guys know it's gone?"

"They're in the dark, Dad. I'm not stupid."

Cue an even longer silence.

"John, you're definitely safe?"

"Yes."

"I'm picking you up right now. Ceri too. Then I'm phoning the bizzies."

"Are you going to tell them the truth?"

"I'll tell them what I can. Look, we'll need to spend some time before we call the coppers, time to get our stories straight. I don't want to draw any more heat than I need to."

"I'll find out the address here and text you."

Dad's breath shuddered through the speaker. "I thought I was done with this crap."

"Dad, you're the one who got us into this *crap*."

"You're right. This is down to me. Once you get involved in the life, it's hard to claw your way out. Text me that address as soon as you've got it. Stay safe."

"You too, Dad. You too."

I filled in the details of the conversation Ceri hadn't been able to work out for herself. She finally seemed resigned to going back to Greenways.

Dream over.

186

"It's kind of sad, though."

"You mean you enjoyed going on the run with me?"

Her eyes smiled. "I did. Yes."

She gave me a hug and I hugged back.

"It had to end some time," I said. "Do you know the address of this place?"

Ceri thought then shook her head.

"I heard somebody say it, but I don't remember. We'll ask in a minute. Talk to me first."

Mop came over. "Hey, John, are you done with my phone?"

I handed it over. "Can I have another borrow in a minute?"

He nodded. "No sweat. I'll be over there."

Ceri watched him go. "He's all right. They all are. We got lucky."

"Good job I burned that guy's *Sun*."

"That was fun."

"Yes, I wish I could have Snapchatted his face."

We sat side by side on the landing, backs to the wall. She nudged me.

"Are you OK?"

"As good as I can be . . . in the circumstances."

"Right."

She glanced into the living room. The place was filling up. There were some crates of booze and Mop was hooking up the speakers.

"The party's about to start."

Ceri nodded. "I wish we could stay. Are you in the mood?"

"Not really. You?"

"Yes. It's as if my life has started over. Since my nan got ill, I've been living like a zombie." She stuck out her arms. "Grr. Ah."

I looked into her hazel eyes. She might not be interested in me, but I was still interested in her.

"It hasn't though, has it? I mean, this little adventure of ours, whatever it is, it's coming to an end."

"What did your dad say about the killing? How much does he know?"

"He didn't have much to say. He thought the phone might be bugged."

Ceri stared.

"You're making it up!"

"I wish I was," I said. "Did you know we were the subject of a manhunt?"

"You're kidding!"

"I suppose we should have expected it. We're on the news. You're a star, Ceri James."

Instinctively, Ceri glanced at the partygoers. "Nobody's said anything."

"Maybe they don't follow the news. This is the counter culture."

Ceri slipped her right foot from her flip-flop and flexed her toes.

"I wish I had some proper shoes. Some dope has already

trodden on me." She rested her head on my shoulder. "I should call my nan."

"We'll get Mop's phone in a minute."

Ceri nodded. "It feels weird. I mean, here we are, at a party, and somewhere out there things are going to crap."

"Scary, isn't it?"

"Dead scary. It's like a war with three sides, the good guys, the bad guys and the police."

I rubbed my chin on the top of her head. "All that stuff, I can't believe it happened."

I thought about Wales. There were times it felt like a love story. There were times I could have killed her. Why did it have to be so confusing? Then something happened. The tumblers started to fall into place.

"Ceri, how did you know where to find Bethan?"

She did a double take. "How do you mean?"

"You were last there when you were ten. Kids don't remember addresses, not after six years."

There was no answer.

"Ceri."

Her admission oozed out like toothpaste.

"I looked it up. When you were asleep."

"You used my computer? You went on the internet?"

She nodded.

"And I spoke to Gemma."

I stared in disbelief. "You're kidding!"

Dropped eyes. "No."

"That's it, then. Everything falls into place. A few words

from Gemma and a quick search of the Google history on my PC, that's how they found us in Lodgie, that's how they found us in Wales. Ceri James, you're a screw-up."

"It wasn't Gemma. I only told her a few details."

"So who else was it? It all fits."

Ceri was at her most stubborn.

"She wouldn't betray me."

"She did though, didn't she?"

She stared past me. "I won't believe it."

I finally locked on to her gaze. "You believe it. I can see it in your face."

There was another silence then a hard, stubborn look came into her eyes.

"I'm going to see her, have it out with her."

"What?"

"I have to know what she's done. Did they threaten her? If she betrayed me, I have to know. I have to see her."

"Are you crazy? What if she blows you up to those guys? We can't be sure what's happening. We can't trust anybody."

Ceri's eyes welled with tears. "She fingered me to those animals. She told them where to find me. Why would she do that? She's my best friend."

"My guess is Snakehead's a persuasive kind of guy," I said. "You said yourself she's desperate for money."

Ceri rested her forehead on her knees. I was about to say something when Freya appeared.

"Are you going to sit there all evening? There's food."

She moved her body to the music. She moved well. I could see some of the guys looking at her. "There's dancing."

She held out a hand. Ceri hid her tears and took it. I gave a sigh of relief. Freya's appearance seemed to have put an end to Ceri's mad idea about confronting Gemma.

I followed them back to the party. I started to text Dad.

Ceri was happy to hang out with the girls. They sat in a corner, laughing and joking. I can't say I took to Freya: too distant, too critical somehow. No matter what I said or did, she had this way of arching her eyebrows, kind of superior. I kept thinking she was looking down at me. I heard a voice.

"Feeling left out?"

It was Mop.

"A bit."

He saw me watching Ceri. "You like her, don't you?"

I smiled. "I didn't know it showed."

Mop thumped my shoulder. "John, you're an open book. Take it from me, Ceri knows how you feel."

"Sugar," I said. "I just remembered. I was supposed to tell my dad the address here. Where are we?"

Mop slapped the phone in my hand.

"Dad, I'm sorry. I got talking."

"John, are you having a laugh? I thought something had happened. You've got to stop jerking me around. I'm coming now. I'm round Otis's house. I'll be there in a few minutes. No more silly beggars. What's the address?"

I told him. Weird, isn't it? It was as if Ceri and I had been living in some alternative universe. Nothing seemed normal any more.

"Right, be at the front door waiting. What's the time now? Nine o'clock. OK, I'll be there in twenty minutes. Be in the hallway, ready. Keep a look out for the car."

"No problem, Dad, I won't le—"

He cut the call before I could finish. Mop was waiting for his phone back.

"In the doghouse, are you?"

I nodded. "Call me Rover. I've got a feeling there are going to be a lot of questions."

"So you weren't telling us the truth. You are in trouble?"

I wondered how much to say. "Kind of."

"Runaways?"

"Well . . ."

"I know," Mop said. "Kind of. I've been there myself."

"Yeah?"

"When I was fifteen. I had a row with my dad about staying out late. I went missing, only a couple of days. I slept in somebody's outhouse. My folks grounded me for weeks."

I gave the flat a meaningful look. "And now you're strictly legit?"

He laughed. Any other time, I would have asked him to tell me his story, but my thoughts were elsewhere.

"Do you know where Ceri is? She was over in that corner, but she's gone."

Mop looked around. "No idea."

I started to look. Mop came with me. We peered in the kitchen where people were standing talking. A tall blond woman turned and stared. She messed with her phone and showed me a picture.

"Is this you?"

There was my own face staring out at me. I was in the news. Famous. Or was that notorious? There was no point denying it. Dad was on his way so what difference did it make?

"Yes, that's me."

"It says the police are looking for you. What did you do?"

I decided to tough it out.

"I'm a serial killer. I assassinated a guy with a Weetabix."

"Seriously."

"You're right, my weapon of choice is Coco Pops."

"Come . . . on. What did you do? Really."

"Nothing. It's sorted anyway. My dad's coming for me. We're going to talk to the coppers together."

The blonde was half cut and giggling. "It's like meeting a celebrity."

Mop laughed. "Yes, he's a right little Justin Bieber." He clapped his hands and raised his voice. "Anybody seen Ceri?"

That just got him blank looks. Nobody knew who Ceri was.

"What about Freya? They were together."

Bunny appeared through a sea of faces. "They were sitting on the stairs the last time I saw them."

"I'll find them," I told Mop. "You enjoy yourself."

I stuck out a hand.

"Thanks for helping."

Mop told me to forget it and patted my cheek. "Whatever your problem is, I hope you get it sorted."

I nodded. "Me too."

I left him and worked my way through the partygoers. The flat was heaving. Where had all these people come from? For a while I stared at the scene, my first real entrance into the adult world, before continuing my search for Ceri.

There was a crush around the door and I had to explain again that, yes, I was the kid the police were looking for and no, I hadn't done anything wrong and look, I didn't have time to hang around explaining myself. I dragged myself away and pushed through the crush. That's when I spotted Ceri. I detached her from Freya and Sarah. Her face was flushed.

"Have you been drinking?'

"Only a couple of bottles of beer. Maybe three."

Three bottles in such a short time. She was well gone.

"I thought you didn't like the stuff."

"It's a party."

"We've got to go. Dad's on his way."

I led the way outside and we stood on the steps. She was definitely tipsy. I hoped the cool air would sober her up. It didn't work. One minute she was high as a kite, the next she was cranky as hell.

"I don't want to go back to Greenways," she said. "On the run is more fun."

"Ceri," I said. "You're living a fantasy. Nobody can live the way we've been living for the last twenty-four hours."

A cloud came over her.

"What do you know about the way people live? You can't imagine."

That's when I said it.

"You mean Sean."

That one mention by Bethan and it had been rolling round in my head ever since. Who was Sean? What did he do? Ceri's face filled with horror.

"How do you know about Sean? Who told you?"

"Bethan."

Ceri was beside herself.

"She had no right!"

She collapsed into sobs and slumped on to the steps. I sat next to her and tried to comfort her, slipping an arm round her shoulders. Bad move. Did I never learn? She reacted as if touched by a cattle prod.

"Get your hands off me!"

I held up my arms.

"I'm not touching, OK. See, no touching." A thought crossed my mind. "Sean was your mum's boyfriend, wasn't he? Did he . . . did he interfere with you?"

More sobbing then a nod.

"He'd been trying it on for weeks. I was so scared. Whenever Mum was out he would come to my room."

I remembered the way she kicked off right out of the blue. Now it made sense.

"Christ, Ceri, I'm sorry."

"He didn't do anything," she said.

"I thought you said . . ."

"He tried to. He came to my room when we were at Bethan's."

"Are you messing? You were only ten."

"That doesn't matter with men like Sean. Mum must have been asleep. I started screaming. Bethan came and told him to get out of her house. She was great, just like when she fought with those animals yesterday." She looked away. "Not like my mum."

"What do you mean?"

"It's as if she was under Sean's spell," Ceri said. "She believed him over her own daughter."

I just stared while she continued. She leaned against me and wept, more gently than before. Ceri had been places in her life no kid should go. I heard a car engine. Headlights flashed and I peered through the dark. It was Dad. Otis was in the passenger seat. Ceri was still talking, oblivious to the vehicle.

"Bethan called the police," she said. "Mum begged her not to. She said it was a misunderstanding. Do you believe that? I needed my mum to be there for me."

"Didn't the police investigate?"

"They picked Sean up and interviewed him. Mum spoke up for him. She made me say I'd been lying."

"Your own mum did that!"

Ceri nodded miserably.

"She called me a bitch for telling on Sean. It didn't do her any good. Sean walked out on her like all the others. Mum ended up so far gone, I had to go and live with my nan. When she got sick, I went into care." Her eyes widened. "I never phoned to see how she was."

Dad shouted from the car. "Are you coming?"

"Give me a moment, yeah?" I gave Ceri a reassuring smile. "You can use my dad's phone."

"Everybody lets me down," Ceri said. "Mum, Gemma, even Bethan. Why did she have to tell you about Sean?"

"Don't hold it against her," I said. "She was worried he might still be around."

I'm not sure I got through to her. Dad was getting impatient.

"For goodness' sake, John."

I walked over and leaned in the window.

"Just give me a moment, will you? Things have been kicking off."

"You've got one minute. There's been enough messing about."

"I know, Dad, I know, but you have to understand. This hasn't been easy for me either."

"Just hurry up. I'm running out of patience."

"Sorry, Ceri's upset about something."

Dad looked past me.

"Where is she?"

I spun round and saw the empty space where Ceri had been sitting.

A shiver ran down my spine.

One of the partygoers was smoking on the steps.

"Did you see the girl who was here?"

"Yes, she went that way, you know, to the top of the road. She hailed a cab."

"Where the hell is she now?" My blood ran cold as an idea squirmed into my mind. I imagined Ceri knocking on Gemma's door. She had a death wish.

"She didn't have any money," I said. "How could she get a taxi?"

Then I remembered. She had the change from the train ticket. Without another word, I turned and raced over to the car and pounded on the window.

"We've got to go. Now!"

"What in God's name are you talking about?"

I scrambled into the back seat and buckled up.

"What now?" Otis demanded. "I thought this mess was finally sorted. Where's the girl?"

I could only think of one place she might go. Gemma's.

"That's what I'm telling you. She's gone. I think I know where. She mentioned the estate where Gemma lives. Ceri's got this mad idea in her head. She could be in danger."

Otis looked at Dad. "Do you know what he's talking about?"

Dad looked as clueless as Otis. "No."

"Just drive," I said, "and phone the police. I'll explain on the way."

Dad bombed down the Dock Road on the way north. The night wrapped itself round us like a glove. There were no traffic lights, no speed cameras, nothing to slow us down. There was hardly a vehicle to hold us up. Otis made the call to the police and palmed the phone.

"What's Gemma's address?"

I stared out at the looming mass of a scrapyard. "Ceri mentioned the name of the estate."

"That's it?"

"That's all I know." I struggled to remember something, anything that might help. "I'll do my best to explain where it is."

We sped past a moored vessel. Its lights were gleaming in the night. I love Liverpool after dark, but this was one night when I hated every single thing I saw. It all looked menacing and alien, a hostile landscape that hid danger in its dark folds. Dad hung a right on to Millers Bridge then a left, accelerating past the squat terraced housing and car dealerships. He had a question.

"What's this this Gemma like? Is she dangerous?"

"I don't know. Not dangerous, I don't think. Easily led. I think she might have grassed Ceri out."

Otis rubbed his nose. "People do desperate things when they've got no money."

"What if she calls Snakehead?"

Dad and Otis swapped glances. It didn't take a genius to realise they knew who I was talking about. There was something they weren't telling me.

"What?"

"This Snakehead," Dad said. "I know him. At least, I know his reputation."

This was the last thing I needed.

"Is there a single lowlife you don't know?"

Dad let the comment go.

"His real name's Paul Holligan. When there was that straightener, he was the enforcer on the other side."

"And? Stop holding out on me, Dad. What else?"

"Holligan's a psycho among psychos. People have been saying it for years. The clothes he wears, the car he drives, they mark him out. He thinks he's fireproof. He just doesn't care. It's a wonder he's survived this long."

I could feel a stream of ice stealing down my spine.

"Why are you telling me this?"

"You need to know how crazy he is," Dad said. "He battered a guy within an inch of his life then he returned to the same location to do the same thing to another man. The only reason he didn't do time was he made the witnesses disappear. He's territorial, a creature of habit. The word on the street is, if his enemies don't pop him, his own side will."

So that was the state of play. Snakehead was a bomb primed to explode and Ceri was rushing into the circle of devastation.

"What you're telling me," I said, knowing the answer even before the words were out of my mouth, "is that Snakehead will keep coming after us, no matter what the risk? He's got nothing holding him back."

"That's exactly what I'm saying. Dealing with your regular villains is bad enough. This guy, he's a renegade. He's that mad I wouldn't put it past him to pop somebody right outside a cop shop."

A renegade. There was no limit to what he might do. This was never going to end. The vehicle slowed.

"Is this it? Is this the right estate?"

I craned to see. A fine drizzle was falling and it made everything misty. There wasn't a soul around.

"Do you have any details? Street name? House number?"

"Nothing. Keep driving round."

Bleary street lights washed through the dark. We cruised the deserted streets.

"This is hopeless," Otis growled.

"We can't give up."

Dad reassured me. "Nobody's giving up."

That's when we saw her. I recognised her immediately from the photo Ceri had showed me.

Gemma.

Mousey hair, slightly chubby features, glasses. She was slumped against a garden fence. We screamed to a halt.

"Where is she?" I demanded. "Where's Ceri?"

Dad joined me. Gemma stared, wondering who we were.

"Listen to me, Gemma. I'm John. I've been with Ceri the last few days."

Gemma came out of her daze. "She said."

"OK, Gemma, now focus. Where's Ceri? She's in trouble and I think you're part of the problem."

Gemma started sobbing.

Her face crumpled into a mask of misery and self-pity. "I kept telling Paul I didn't know where Ceri was, but he wouldn't believe me. He kept coming round, pestering me. We were having another argument when Ceri turned up. I didn't want any of this to happen."

"This isn't about you," I told her. "Where did they take Ceri?"

She shook her head. "I don't know."

"You've got to help us."

"I told you. I don't know where she is." Suddenly she was focused, desperate to help. "They only just went. You might still catch them."

That gave me hope.

"Which way?"

She pointed.

"What was Snakehead driving?"

Gemma stared. "Snakehead? What are you talking about?"

"Paul Holligan," Dad explained. "What kind of car was he in?"

"Oh, it was fancy, a big car. I've never seen one like it."

"Blue?"

"Yes, blue."

"It's the Lincoln," I said. "Got to be."

"Right," Dad said. "Let's go."

As we clambered into the car, I noticed something. Otis had his phone in his hand and a look on his face that said he had something to hide. When you grow up among lies, you get to know the signs. There was no time to ask who he had been calling.

The estate was a maze of red-brick houses. Some of the streets were laid out in a circular pattern making it difficult for strangers to negotiate their way out.

"How the hell do you get out of this place?" Dad growled.

"Don't complain," Otis said, searching the rain-slicked streets for some sign of a blue Lincoln. "With any luck, Holligan might be having the same problem. It's our only chance."

We hung a left then a right. Dad punched the dash.

"It's like a maze."

"Keep a lid on it," Otis said. "We won't get anywhere shouting and yelling."

That's when I saw the car.

"There! Just going across that junction."

Dad clocked the Lincoln and followed.

"You've got to go faster."

"Worst thing we could do. They'll realise they're being followed. We can't rush this."

"We could lose them."

Dad's face was set. "I won't lose them."

"So what do we do?"

Dad's words came out slow. There was no reassurance.

"I wish I knew. We keep them in sight. It's our only option."

I heard my own voice and couldn't believe what I was saying.

"We should phone the police."

I sounded like Ceri before she got the freedom bug.

"How can we?" Dad said. "You know what Holligan threatened to do if we said anything to the coppers. Do you really want to risk your mum and Trinity's lives?"

Otis had nothing to add. I got it. Where we came from, you didn't talk to the police if you could help it.

So we drove.

And drove.

The Lincoln led us back in the direction of the Dock Road. Dad pulled up at a Give Way sign and peered down the road after the Lincoln. He killed the lights.

"What are you doing?"

"On a busy dual carriageway, we might not get noticed. Here . . ." His voice trailed off for a moment. "We're too conspicuous."

He turned out of the side road, real slow, rolling forward down the Dock Road.

"Dad, you're going to lose them."

Otis had his hand on my shoulder. "Trust him. Your dad knows what he's doing."

I looked at the two men: my dad and a guy who was closer than any family. You know what? At that moment, I don't think I knew either of them. The Lincoln pulled into a deserted dock complex. Liverpool's changed since it was a busy port. Some of the hulking warehouses have been turned into tourist attractions, shops, hotels, but these buildings were deserted, silent and unlit.

"Is this where they've got Mum and Trinity?" I asked.

Dad nodded. "This is it."

He pulled forward so he could look through the gate and into the windswept open space. The waters in the dock gleamed like beaten bronze in the moonlight.

"They must've paid off the security guys," he murmured. He came to a decision. "You stay here with Otis."

"What are you going to do?"

"I'm going to settle this for good and all."

"Dad, what's all this about?"

That's when he reached inside the glove compartment. He unwrapped a cloth to reveal a handgun. My skin crawled.

"What are you doing with that?"

"I'm going to get my family."

So that crap about going straight, all those promises, they were all lies.

"You said you were finished with this. You promised."

He leaned in close and wrapped a hand round my neck, pressing his forehead against mine. "I never lied to you," he said. "When I told you I was done with all this, I was telling the truth."

"Dad, you've got a gun."

"It belongs to Leroy. I held it for him."

Otis spoke for the first time. Anger was written into his features.

"This is your idea of leaving the life behind? You hold a gun for a man?"

Dad looked like he'd been slapped.

"I hid it for him, the gun, a fake passport, some cash, in case he had to leave in a hurry." He shook his head as if trying to banish ghosts. "Listen, that night when they shot up the house, the reason I was able to get the family out before it happened was Leroy warned me in advance. I owed him."

Otis glared. "You owed him nothing. Leroy knew the risks. The only responsibility you ever had was to your family."

Dad held his gaze. "Leroy stuck his neck out. He saved my family. Maybe I was right. Maybe I was wrong. Either way, I've found the only people who really matter to me and it's down to me to get them out."

My heart was slamming. "Dad, what are you going to do?"

He checked the gun's chamber.

"I told you, whatever it takes to bring them home."

"But . . ."

Then I got it. He was bringing Mum and Trinity home even if it cost him his own freedom. He went to get out of the car, but Otis pulled him back with a strong arm.

"You're going nowhere," he snarled. "There's things you don't understand."

"What do you think you're doing?" Dad demanded.

"You do what I say and stay put," Otis ordered.

Dad tried to wriggle out of Otis's grasp, but Otis was the stronger man. The explanation for his behaviour came moments later when three police vans swept into sight. An unmarked car followed. I recognised the livery. Matrix. Merseyside police's armed response unit. Dad turned.

"Otis? What is this?"

"Stay here. Explanations later."

Otis was out of the car. He walked over to the unmarked vehicle as it pulled up opposite. He leaned through the passenger side window. One thing was for sure, he knew the guys inside.

"Dad," I said, "what's happening?"

The look on his face said he knew no more than I did. The conversation continued in front of us then Otis straightened up and walked briskly over. He got back in the car.

"We stay put," he said.

Dad wasn't about to accept anything on trust.

"I don't take any orders until I know what's happening," he said. "What gives, Ote? How did the police know where to come?" He let the ideas fall into place. "Oh hell, no. You're in some copper's pocket."

Otis jabbed a finger into Dad's chest.

"Are you judging me, boy? You think being a gangster is better than being a grass."

Now I got it.

"You're an informer?" I groaned. "How long?"

"Your old fella's not the only stupid kid to go wrong. I wasn't always a *pillar of the community*. That's right, I did some stupid things back in the day. I was facing jail time and this copper cuts me a deal. It gets me a suspended sentence. I feed him information and I stay a free man. Well, what would you do?"

Dad was thunderstruck.

"All these years and none of us knew."

"That's right," Otis said. "None of you knew." He pounded his fist on the dash. "You know why, because I didn't want you to. I kept my secret in here." His hand moved to his forehead. "You think I'm some kind of traitor? Grow up, lad. I'm a survivor. I did what I had to do."

"Did they pay you?"

Otis turned my way. "What?"

"The police. Did they pay you?"

There was a delay, then the answer.

"Yes, I got paid."

"That's how you started your business, isn't it?"

Otis was watching the police moving into position.

"I worked hard to get my business going."

Dad joined in. "The money must have helped."

Otis folded his arms. "You can think what you want of me. I saved your skin more than once. You know what the coppers are? Contacts. Contacts is why you're not inside." The wind gusted outside then he spoke again. "You give me that gun. You give me everything you held for Leroy, you get me?"

"I'm not handing anything over to the police."

Otis looked angry. "You don't know me, do you? None of this stuff goes to the police. I'll make it vanish then you're in the clear."

"Your friends in blue will let you do that?" Dad asked.

"Are you having a laugh? I've got no special privileges. If the bizzies see what we've got here in this car, we both go down."

I listened. It was as if I was staring through a window into an alien world. Dad could barely look Otis in the eye.

"Well," Otis said. "Are you going to let the police do their thing?"

"Looks like I don't have any choice," Dad said. He shifted slowly in his seat. "I don't think I know you at all."

Otis shrugged. "You know me. You just don't know all

of me. Don't judge me. Sometimes all you've got is bad choices. I did what I had to do. Now be smart for once in your life and let's hope things work out."

Suddenly there was a loud pop, followed by a lot of shouting. Dad was out of the car before anybody could stop him, running towards the gate.

"Oh my God! Oh my God!"

Two officers tried to stop him but he barged past them. That's when I saw Mum and Trinity being rushed towards a van. Beyond them, somebody was on the ground with his arms behind his back. It looked like Fat Lad. His head was jerking about as he struggled.

"Where's Snakehead? Do you see Holligan?"

Dad had Mum and Trinity in his arms. The police were shouting something and he was shoving them away. Everything was so confused. Mum saw me and yelled.

"John! Oh, thank God. John."

"Mum, are you all right?"

"We're fine."

I was out of the car and running. I didn't reach them. Before I could get to the police cordon, there was a scream. I spun round, my gaze sweeping across the vast open space before the warehouses. Then there they were. Snakehead had Ceri and he was running, dragging her with him.

"There!" I yelled. "There."

Voices were exploding around me, the gruff commands of the police, the desperate screams of Mum and Trinity. I scrambled back into the car next to Otis.

"Go!" I yelled. "They're getting away."

Otis turned in the direction of the police.

"Are you messing?" I cried. "You're waiting for orders. They'll be gone."

I saw the way Otis's gaze shifted towards the glove compartment and the gun. He was weighing up his options.

"Snakehead's crazy," I cried. "We have to go after him."

Otis made up his mind.

"You'd better let me in the driver's seat," he growled.

I realised what I'd done, jumping in where Dad had been. We swapped places. The tyres screamed. Behind us one of the vans and the unmarked car were moving, their headlights slashing the darkness. The Lincoln was already out of sight.

"We've lost them!" I bawled.

"Stop shouting," Otis warned. "How do you expect me to concentrate?"

The dark was all around us and there was no sign of the Lincoln's tail lights.

"He's pulled your dad's trick," Otis said. "He's driving without lights."

"You're slowing down," I protested. "Why are you slowing down?"

"I've been avoiding doing this."

I frowned a question.

"I got Holligan's number from a guy so we could make the exchange."

He made the call.

"I think you know me. Yes, that's right. We need to talk." He turned to me. "He hung up."

Moments later, his phone rang.

"Yes?"

He mouthed a name. *Holligan.*

I tried to follow the exchange. Otis hung up and put his foot on the gas.

"What did he say?"

"Crosby beach."

It made sense.

"A creature of habit," I said. "That's what you and Dad said. Crosby beach. He's taking Ceri back to where it all began."

"And he wants you there. I don't like this."

"We both know what he wants," I replied.

It didn't take a genius. With a good brief, he might just get off on the kidnap charge or at least get a short sentence. No way would a guy like Fat Lad grass. Ceri and I were the ones who could put Snakehead inside and he thought we had the evidence to do it.

"The memory card's definitely ruined?" Otis asked.

"Completely wrecked."

He cursed.

"This just gets better." He put his foot down. "Do you know what happened to Holligan's oppo?"

"Fat lad? He was on the floor."

"You sure about that?"

212

"Positive. The coppers have got him. I saw it with my own eyes. Why?"

"I need to know what we're getting into, how many men we're dealing with."

"One."

Except he was one of the biggest psychos in the city.

Just then, the phone rang. Otis picked up, consulted the screen and shoved the phone back in his jacket, unanswered.

"Who was that?"

"Who do you think?"

"Your copper friends?"

"Got it in one."

I frowned. One minute he was the coppers' friend, the next he was blanking them. Otis must have read my mind.

"Think about it, John lad. Thanks to your dad, there's a gun in this vehicle. That's a five-year mandatory sentence."

"But you've been passing the coppers information."

Otis laughed. "You think that makes me immune from prosecution?"

My heart skipped. Five minutes earlier, he was a traitor. Now he was the guy I'd known all my life, trusted, reliable and he was heading into a situation that could see him go down for a long time.

"Do you see the police?" he asked.

I craned my neck. "They're way back."

Otis swung the wheel, throwing me against the door.

Another swing of the wheel and we were roaring down a side street, darkened buildings flashing past.

"Are you trying to kill us?" I yelled.

"I'm trying to lose the police, give myself a breathing space. Whatever happens on the beach, I can't let them find me with that gun."

"So get rid of it now," I suggested.

"And go up against your friend Snakehead unarmed?" He shook his head. "No can do."

The phone went again.

"I bet that's Dad."

"Got it in one. You want to talk to him?"

I shook my head.

"Let's get Ceri."

The car park was deserted. We started to run towards the dunes. All my life, Otis had been the solid guy, completely reliable, composed, confident. Not now. He looked like he was coming apart at the seams.

"You've done your bit," Otis said. "You need to stay in the car."

"No way."

"Stay in the car!"

"What are you going to do, Otis? Hit me?"

"You're your father's son, all right."

Instinctively, I found myself looking in the direction of my house.

"We've all got a lot to lose," Otis said. "All of us. I could still get rid of the gun and hand this situation over to the coppers."

"I see them," I said.

Up ahead, a pair of figures was passing between the dunes. The beach and the bay lay before them under the velvet sky.

"That's them." I grabbed his sleeve. "Otis, we've got to do something."

A backward glance said the police still hadn't found us. Otis's expression was grim.

"You're right. Let's go get your girl."

There was no protest from me. I didn't tell him that Ceri wasn't my girl. What was the point? The iron men were waiting, stark and silent in the gloom. I'd lost sight of Ceri and Snakehead.

"Do you see them?" I asked.

Otis shook his head. "I don't like this."

"You think I do?" I answered. "We didn't ask for this to happen, me or Ceri."

He nodded. "Point taken."

We made our way down to the beach.

"I still don't see them," Otis said. There was mist and light rain on the sands. He continued to search the murk. "John, go back to the car. Please."

"Snakehead won't show himself unless he sees me."

Otis fixed me with a look, thinking about it. Then he relented.

"You're right. Hold on a minute."

"Have you seen something?"

Otis nodded in the direction of the iron men. "Got them."

Snakehead came out from behind one of the statues, lean arm wrapped around Ceri. He was looking our way. As we moved steadily towards him, I became aware of a loud, metallic roar. A helicopter.

"Eye in the sky," Otis observed grimly. He turned towards me. "If I'm found with this gun, I'm going down for a long time."

"It's not about you," I snapped.

He squeezed the bridge of his nose.

"It's about all of us." He rubbed his head thoughtfully. "This is bad."

We were now within shouting distance of Snakehead and Ceri.

"Let her go," I pleaded. "It's over . . ." I forced myself to use Holligan's name. A moment of pure genius. "Paul, I gave the police the memory card."

That's when Snakehead did something I hadn't expected in my worst nightmares.

He grinned.

Not pure genius at all.

"Then I've nothing to lose, have I? You know what's left, soft lad? Work it out."

He let me wonder for another few moments then he spelt it out. "I want revenge."

Then I was reliving the nightmare on the beach. He

had his arm outstretched and I was staring right down the barrel of the gun.

"You and your camera," he said. "You just had to be there, didn't you? That's what brings me down, a couple of stupid kids."

I could sense Otis moving away. Snakehead saw the movement too. Otis was producing his own gun. That did it. Snakehead fired and Otis was on the ground.

"Ote!"

In the slo-mo horror of the moment, my first reaction was to help Otis. It all happened so fast. Ceri was the one who made the difference. With Snakehead distracted, she sank her teeth into his hand. Did Snakehead make a sound? I don't remember. I made enough noise for the both of us. I let out a howl of rage and went for him, slamming into him and sending him crashing backwards on to the sand. Then we were fighting, all three of us. Even with two on one, it was an unequal struggle. Snakehead tossed Ceri to one side like a rag doll. She came back at him, but this time he sent her crashing to the sand with a backhanded slap. I saw blood on his knuckles. Twisting round, he butted me right between the eyes and the world became a blur, a numb, sick blur. But I didn't let go. I kept clawing at him, trying to wrestle him to the ground. It was a losing battle. I could hardly see and I was eating sand. He had me face down. Through the haze came the sound of Ceri's voice. Whatever she said did the trick. I felt Snakehead's grip loosen then he was gone.

"John, are you OK?"

It took me a few moments to focus on her face.

"Snakehead?"

"The coppers are here. He's gone." She pointed. "There."

I saw Snakehead's shadowy form stumbling away. Armed officers were closing in on him. That's when I remembered Otis. I crawled over to him.

"Ote."

He groaned.

"You OK?"

He nodded through the pain. "Shoulder. I'll live." He didn't care about the pain or the blood. "Get shut of the gun. I can't go inside. I can't."

Ceri looked confused.

"Distract the coppers," I said. "There's something I have to do."

I took the weapon from Otis and shoved it in my belt, covering it with my jacket. My legs were unsteady, but I lurched away, gradually recovering my strength. I heard a yell, but I kept going, across the beach, up the steps, slipping on seaweed, and plunged into the dunes. I searched for some sign of the police, but they all seemed to be focused on Snakehead.

There was another shout. Was it directed at me? A figure lurched at the edge of my vision.

I was staggering in the dark, ploughing through the dry, loose sand. I had only one thought in my mind, to get rid of the gun. I found myself on open ground. I felt sick, but I kept going. Was anybody following? I reeled round. There was nobody in sight. Finally, I reached my target, the pond. I hurled the gun right into the middle and heard the splash. So there I stood, sucking in lungfuls of air, praying that nobody had seen me. Time slipped by. The wind boomed. High above, the helicopter roared. Still, there was nobody in sight.

"OK," I told myself. "You've done good."

I had to move. I couldn't do anything to attract the police to the pond. I started to make my way back towards the beach. That's where I saw the armed officer.

"John Bankole?"

"That's right."

"We've been looking for you. What are you doing here?"

It was hard to know how to answer. I eventually came up with a reply of sorts.

"I panicked." I qualified the statement. "When the gun went off, I just ran."

The cop barely reacted.

"Come with me."

There were lights, a silhouetted figure, the continuing, deafening snarl of the chopper.

"Otis?" I asked.

Ceri was in front of me, wrapped in a foil blanket.

"Otis."

"He's OK. They're taking him to hospital."

"And Snakehead?"

"Dead. He fired at the coppers. I saw him fall."

Weird thing, endings. All that time, Snakehead had seemed invincible. Now he was a lump of meat in a body bag. Shot while trying to escape. Only I don't believe that. He hated us and he hated the coppers. I think his hatred of the coppers came out on top. He left the world as a caricature of the gangster.

You don't take me alive.

Ceri went to speak again, but I pulled her to me and hissed into her ear.

"There was only one gun," I told her. "Snakehead's. Only one gun. Get it?"

She breathed her answer back at me.

"Got it."

Otis lived.

Of course he did. He's tough as old boots, Otis, and he's got way more soul. They had to dig a bullet out of his shoulder. He had some sleepless nights, probably more about Dad's gun than the pain. I visited him in hospital and he gave me the most intense third degree in history. Did anybody see me down by the pond? How far did I throw the gun? How deep was the pond anyway? Did they ever drag it?

We never found out the answers to the last two questions, but there's been no comeback. Otis is a free man and he's gone back to his life as a legit businessman. I don't think the police use him any more. They know there was something fishy about the events of that night, but they don't have any evidence. I haven't seen Otis in a while. Him and Dad aren't speaking. You could say relations are strained.

As to Mum and Dad, they split up. They do that. At least once a year. Even when Mum threw him out *for the last time* I knew he'd be back. Trinity sobbed her eyes out when Dad walked out of the door with his suitcase. She was young enough and naïve enough to think it was for keeps. Me, I'd seen it all before. Dad moved back three weeks ago when the Doha contract finished. He was banished from the house for five months, a world record for this family. The night he moved back in, I had a question for him.

"It's over, yeah? No more guns. No more gangs."

"It's been over for years," he said.

"So you said last time."

"I did a favour for a man who saved my family."

I gave him the evil eye. "So who else do you owe favours to?"

He folded his arms. "Nobody."

"And I'm supposed to take it on trust."

He gave a helpless shrug. "What am I supposed to say?"

"Nothing," I told him. "You're good at talking. Not so good at the truth."

"So what do I do to make it right?"

"Nothing," I said. "You do nothing. Nothing iffy, nothing criminal. Just nothing."

He nodded slowly. "I can do that."

And so far he has.

That just leaves Ceri.

She was out of school for a while, a week, maybe more. When she came back, she didn't say much. It felt as if we'd gone back to being strangers. She returned to being the loner she had always been. I ached to talk to her, but she didn't want to know. Every time I went near, she found an excuse to get away. It lasted into spring. It lasted until my GCSEs. You won't credit it, but I didn't try to chat up a girl for two months. I had unfinished business and that was Ceri.

Come the end of the school year, I was ready to put her behind me, move on and accept that a page had been turned. I was moving on to Sixth Form College. Ceri wasn't around after that. Somebody said she'd moved. I called in at Greenways, but they couldn't tell me anything, only that Ceri had relocated. I didn't have a clue where she was or what she had planned for the rest of her life.

Until that Thursday in August, results day, the 25th.

"Hello, stranger."

I turned round and there was Ceri. She looked good, more grown up, more assured. There's a word for that. Happy. She had her results envelope in her hand. It was good to see her smile.

"How did you do?" I asked. "In the exams, I mean."

Even as I put my question, I became aware that she wasn't on her own. There was a woman in her late fifties or early sixties, linking arms with Ceri. She saw me looking.

"Oh, this is my nan."

I remembered everything Ceri had said about her. For a dead woman, she looked in rude, good health.

Nan smiled. "I'm Sal."

I was uncertain what to say next, but eventually I managed a few words.

"You look well," I said.

"I am, thank you," she replied. "I'm in remission. No sign of the cancer any more. It's quite a relief."

"That's great," I said. "Ceri's told me all about you."

I felt awkward. Ceri stepped in.

"That's where I've been," she said. "I've moved back in with Nan. Life's back to normal."

She squeezed Sal's arm. Ceri's love for this woman oozed out of her.

"No more Greenways then?"

"That's right," Ceri answered. "The guys there did their best, but it was never home."

Then she did something I didn't expect. She stepped forward and hugged me, planting a kiss on my cheek. Instinctively, I kind of moved towards her, but she flicked a glance in the direction of her nan.

"I never thanked you," she said.

"Thank me?" I mumbled. "What for?"

"You came for me," she said. "Anything could have happened, but you didn't think twice."

I fielded her thanks. "I couldn't have done it without Otis."

"Families, eh?" Ceri said. "Complicated, aren't they?"

"Have you seen your mum?" I asked.

For a moment I saw the old, scared Ceri showing through.

"I've seen her," she said. "Twice. She's trying to get her life back together. It's slow, you know."

How was I supposed to respond? This was the woman who had hit Ceri, neglected her, sold her little dog, broken her heart over and over again. I took my lead from Ceri.

I was still uncomfortable, but I managed a reply. "I hope things work out."

Ceri's gaze moved to Sal.

"Could you give us a few minutes?" she asked.

Sal nodded. "I'll be in the Tea Room. Join me there when you're ready."

Ceri and I found an empty bench in the school grounds.

"This is a turn-up," I said. "So your mum, is she . . .?"

I hesitated to finish the sentence.

"She's clean," Ceri said. "She hasn't used in nearly a year. She wants to find a way back into my life."

After everything we'd been through, I still felt protective of Ceri.

"Is that a good idea?"

She took my hand. "I'm not a little kid any more. She hurt me. Trust is something you earn. I thought you'd know that with your dad." She tucked a lock of hair behind

224

her ear. She'd let it grow long. "Let's say I'm willing to listen. My nan is my rock. She'll be there even if Mum messes up."

"You don't resent her?"

"There are times when I hate her. You don't forget all that stuff easily, but she's my mum, John. I want to be able to love her. I really do."

I remembered the envelope in her hand. "So how were your results?"

"Fantastic. Way better than I expected. I'm going to Sixth Form College. I want to do Health and Social Care at uni. What about you?"

"Not bad," I said. "Not bad at all. Good enough to go on to A level."

"Any plans?"

I couldn't help myself. I burst out laughing.

"Did I ever come across as somebody with plans?" I asked. "No, I'm weighing my options as they say."

We both remembered our crazy time.

"Can you believe what we did?" she asked. "There's something called chaos theory. That was us. Were we selfish, worrying everybody like that?"

I shrugged. "I don't think we had much choice. It all made sense at the time."

Suddenly, Ceri's face lit up. "I'm getting a puppy."

"Yes? That's great. Have you got a name for it?"

"She's a pug. I'm calling her Tyke. Tilly Mint was my second choice."

I laughed. "Figures. Have you been in touch with Bethan?"

"She's good. We went to see her two weeks ago, to thank her for everything she did." Ceri fiddled with her phone. "I called on the guy whose car we took. He was really nice about it. Did you know Snakehead threatened his little girl?"

"That's the kind of thing scum like him would do."

Ceri's face clouded a little. "Has there been any comeback after what happened?"

"Fat lad was in the *Echo*. Sentencing next week."

"What'll he get?"

"My dad reckons he'll do eight years inside."

Ceri went quiet for a while.

"What about Gemma?" I asked.

"No," she said. "That's a step too far. We've gone our separate ways."

To our left, a few of the girls were hugging and squealing with delight over their results. I ached to hold Ceri. I glanced at the girls.

Ceri let me take her hand and smiled.

Then I had my arms around her. Our cheeks brushed and her lips found mine, soft and urgent. It only lasted seconds. I could feel her heart beating against my chest, her warm breath on my mouth. Then we pulled back.

"See you," she said breezily.

"Yes, see you."

I was halfway home when I felt the piece of paper in

my pocket. It reminded me of Leroy Brown. I took it out. There was an address and phone number.

Ceri's. She must have passed it to me during the kiss. Even when I thought I'd got to know Ceri, she never failed to surprise. Maybe I would never really work her out.

I smiled and spoke out loud.

"Well, well, looks like I could be seeing you sooner rather than later, Ceri James."

About the Author

Alan Gibbons is a full-time writer and a visiting speaker and lecturer at schools, colleges and literary events nationwide, including the major book festivals: Edinburgh, Northern Children's Book Festival, Swansea, Cheltenham, Sheffield and Salford.

Alan was a teacher for eighteen years, and is a key supporter of a high-profile, nationwide campaign to champion libraries and librarianship and to re-evaluate government commitment to educational spending. Alan is an honorary CILIP member and recipient of the Fred and Anne Jarvis Award for services to education, and has won seventeen book awards. He lives in Liverpool with his wife and four children.

Visit Alan's website at www.alangibbons.com, read his blog at alangibbons.net and follow him on Twitter @mygibbo and Facebook at www.facebook.com/alan.gibbons.35

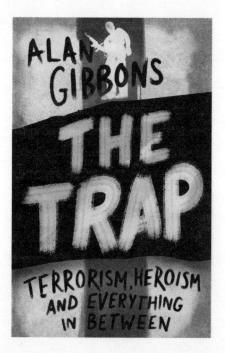

Terrorism, heroism and everything in between . . .

MI5 agent, Kate, receives a tip-off about an asset, who
seems too good to be true. Amir and Nasima are trying
to make friends at their new school but struggling to
keep a terrible secret. A group of jihadists are planning
something. And behind it all stands Majid.
Brother. Son. Hero. Terrorist.

Spanning Iraq, Syria and England, THE TRAP grapples
with one of the greatest challenges of our time.

We've got to go. Now.

It's early morning and Danny's mother is at his bedside,
urging him to get up. They're on the run from Chris,
his mother's boyfriend, a violent man who beats them
both up, and won't let them go.

Chris pursues Danny and his mother from London to the
north, where they take refuge with Danny's grandparents.
But even there, nothing is safe. Danny is conspicuous as
the only mixed-race boy in their small community, and
with the ever-present threat of discovery, he has to
learn how to live continually on the edge.

Would you dare to be different?

ALAN
GIBBONS
HATE

INSPIRED
BY A
TRUE STORY

Eve's older sister, Rosie, was bright and alive and
always loved being the centre of attention. Then one
day, she is brutally murdered. Six months later, Eve
meets Antony and discovers that he was there the
night Rosie died and did nothing to help. Is there
any way she can ever get past that?

Inspired by the tragic murder of Sophie Lancaster, which
saw Sophie and her partner Rob viciously attacked in
Stubbylee Park, Bacup, Lancashire, because of the way
they dressed, this is a hard-hitting real-life thriller about
friendship, courage, loss, forgiveness and about our
society and communities.

'He was here again last night, the man with the dead eyes.
He was in my room and in my head.'

There are not many things Nick Mallory knows for sure.

He knows there was a car crash. He knows he is in
hospital. And he knows he feels furious with his father.
What he doesn't know is why.

As his memories start to return, Nick finds himself
caught in a net of secrets and lies – where truth and
perception collide, and heroes and villains are not
easy to tell apart.